Magic & Mirrors

Starry Hollow Witches, Book 17

Annabel Chase

Red Palm Press LLC

Copyright © 2023 by Annabel Chase

All rights reserved.

No part of this book may be reproduced in any form or by any electronic or mechanical means, including information storage and retrieval systems, without written permission from the author, except for the use of brief quotations in a book review.

 Created with Vellum

Chapter One

What are you staring at? Did you finally notice that wild hair growing out of your cheek?

Startled, I jumped back from the bathroom mirror and turned to regard my raccoon familiar. "You need to start wearing bells so I can hear you coming."

Both practical and festive. Raoul climbed on the toilet tank and perched there. *Seriously, though. You don't normally spend this much time admiring yourself. What's the occasion?*

"Sunday dinner is in two hours, and I want to make sure there's nothing for Aunt Hyacinth to criticize." I grabbed the tweezers and plucked the wayward hair from my cheek. "Like a wild hair."

That's an exercise in futility. Your aunt can always find something to criticize. It's her superpower. What else are you doing?

I gave him an innocent look. "What else could there be?"

I heard you talking to yourself.

"I always talk to myself. It's a sign of intelligence."

It's a sign of lunacy, but we'll set that aside for a minute. He leaned forward and scrutinized me with those bandit eyes. *'Fess up.*

I exhaled, breathing a ring of fog on the mirror that smudged my reflection. "Fine. I'm practicing daily affirmations."

Raoul laughed. *Why would you do that?*

"To help my relationship with Aunt Hyacinth. She's shown a willingness to behave better, but that doesn't mean I shouldn't try to improve too. That way if she reverts to old habits, I won't be so quick to react. I'm responsible for how I respond to her."

Raoul's beady eyes turned to slits. *What have you done with Ember? Is this a body switch-uation because—let's be honest—self-reflection isn't your strong suit.*

"What's that supposed to mean?"

Exactly what I just said. I don't think there was any ambiguity.

"I self-reflect all the time."

Deciding whether you want pepperoni or sausage on your pizza doesn't count as self-reflection.

"The answer to that is always both."

Fair enough.

"Mom, did you wash my blue dress?" Marley's voice rang out from downstairs. "I want to wear it to dinner."

"It's on the drying rack in the kitchen," I yelled.

The piercing bark of a certain aging Yorkshire terrier spiked my blood pressure. Prescott Peabody III, or PP3 as he was regularly known, could shatter glass with his warning cry.

Somebody's at the door. Raoul climbed to the floor and rushed downstairs ahead of me.

"Are you the butler now?" I called after him. He'd kill me in my sleep if I tried to put a bow tie on him.

By the time I arrived at the bottom of the steps, Calla was in the living room chatting with Marley, who held the blue dress draped over her arm.

The crone shifted her wrinkled gaze to me. "You're awfully dressed up for our magic session, duckling."

"We don't have a session today." I cut a quick glance at Marley. "Do we?"

Marley shrugged. "I don't have anything in my planner."

Gnarled fingers scratched the old witch's white hair. "That's odd. I came straight from my dance class because I thought I would be late otherwise."

"We have dinner at Thornhold today," I explained. "I wouldn't typically make plans for Sunday afternoon."

I, for one, would like more information about this dance class, Raoul interrupted.

Calla's face scrunched in a tight ball. "I'm sure it's my mistake. I've been growing more forgetful by the day. My memory potion doesn't seem to work as well as it used to."

I felt a pang of sympathy for the elderly witch. "I'm sure we can squeeze in a quick lesson, if you're up for it. Can't we, Marley?"

Marley nodded with enthusiasm. "You know I'm always interested in learning from the best."

Calla patted Marley's cheek. "Such a butt-kisser. I adore that about you." She pushed up the sleeves of her pink cardigan. "Let's head into the kitchen then, shall we?"

Marley shot me a pointed look. "I'll put the dress in my room and come back."

Calla was already halfway to the kitchen. "Warn me if

your dog comes running so I don't trip over him. I doubt I'll hear him, stealthy little fur ball."

"There's no fear of that," I said. PP3 wasn't much of a runner anymore.

Her gaze swept the room with a slightly imperial air. "Where's your altar, duckling?"

"Right there." I pointed to the far wall.

Calla stooped over the altar that was currently covered in damp clothes. "You're using your altar as a drying rack?"

"I ran out of space. What do you expect me to do?"

"Show a little respect, for starters." She used the tip of her wand to remove the offending items from the altar and placed them on a nearby chair.

"Would you like me to bring in plants from the garden?" Marley asked, appearing behind us.

"I saw your garden on my way in, sweetness. You're doing a magnificent job."

"Thank you, Calla. That means a lot coming from you." Marley beamed with pride. The special herb garden was a labor of love for her. It was the same spot where our ancestor, Ivy Rose, had tended a similar garden long ago.

"I'm glad somebody's interested in what a crone has to say. Lately I feel as though my words fall on closed ears." She sighed in a way that suggested a story.

I glanced at the clock on the microwave and quickly debated whether we had time for a story *and* a lesson. My relationship with Aunt Hyacinth was currently in a good place. I didn't want to jeopardize it by showing up late for dinner.

"What's going on, Calla?" Marley asked.

My daughter clearly didn't share my need to strategize the level of interest to demonstrate.

"First, the herbs," Calla said. "Then we'll talk about my

invisible witch syndrome." She glanced longingly at the counter. "Any chance a crone could trouble you for a nip of brandy or something else to warm the stomach? I seem constantly chilled to the bone these days."

"Oh." I tried to recall what I had in stock. "No brandy, but I have tequila for margaritas."

"I don't need the extra sugar, duckling." She paused. "Just the shot of tequila will be fine."

Okay, not the response I was expecting. "Marley, you get the herbs. I'll handle the alcohol."

I like her style, Raoul said. *Has she always been this interesting?*

Something's clearly troubling her, I replied.

As Marley exited the cottage, I hurried to the cabinet to fetch a shot glass and the bottle of tequila that I'd bought at the Wish Market.

"Unburden yourself, Calla," I said, setting the shot glass in front of her. Hopefully, she'd ignore the shape of boobs protruding from the glass. Raoul had brought the shot glass from the dump as a gift for me, and I didn't have the heart to reject it.

Calla released a deep sigh that suggested a long conversation. I made a mental note of the time. If it turned into a therapy session, I'd have to find a way to eject her without wounding her further.

"My friend Ruby bought me a beautiful silver moon pendant necklace for my birthday," Calla began.

"That doesn't sound bad," I said. I filled her glass with tequila. I was half tempted to pour myself a shot in anticipation of Sunday dinner, but I wasn't keen on alcohol as a coping device unless karaoke was involved.

"No, the necklace itself is lovely." Calla tipped back the boobs and downed the tequila in one gulp, slamming the glass on the table with more gusto than I expected from her arthritic hand. "Ruby noticed I wasn't wearing it the next few times I saw her. Finally, she got angry and demanded to know why. She said if I didn't like it, she would've been happy to exchange it for something else."

"The necklace was a gift," I said. "Why does Ruby have expectations about how it should be enjoyed?"

"I don't blame her, really. She doesn't have much spending money, and I'm sure she thought the necklace was perfect for me, and it is."

"Then what's the issue?" I asked.

Calla gazed at me from beneath hooded eyes. "Promise not to judge me?"

"Of course," I said. "This is a judgment-free household."

Unless you're putting pineapple on pizza, Raoul added. *Then all bets are off.*

Calla stretched out her knobby fingers. "It's my hands. They're not as deft and nimble as they used to be. I can't manage the clasp of the necklace, and I live alone, so I don't have anyone to help me with it."

"What about a spell?" I asked. It seemed like the obvious answer for a witch.

Marley pushed open the door with her back, carrying a tray of small pots. "A spell for what?"

"Calla needs help with fine motor skills," I said. "Know any spells to help with that?"

"I'm sure I knew them once upon a time," Calla said, "but it's so hard to remember everything. My brain seems to prioritize necessities and eliminates the rest."

Sounds like your brain, Raoul told me. *She's ancient. What's your excuse?*

"A friend at the academy showed me a spell that ties his shoelaces for him," Marley said. "I bet that could help you."

Calla lit up. "Yes, I think it would. Thank you for the excellent suggestion, duckling."

Marley set the tray on the table. "It's super easy. Even Kale picked it up right away, and he's the weak link in our class."

Calla smiled. "There's always one."

My gaze cut to the clock. As the minutes ticked by, the knots in my stomach grew. I was turning into Marley. There was no way I could hurry Calla out of the cottage though. She'd already expressed sadness over being an invisible witch, arguing with a friend, losing her memory, and having difficulty with fine motor skills. Only a monster would cut her visit short.

Raoul jumped down from the chair and tugged Calla's hand. *Time to go, crone. Dinner's cooking, and leftovers from a Thornhold Sunday dinner are like nirvana in my mouth.*

Leave her be. I scowled at the raccoon, and he released her hand.

"Does Raoul want to show me something?" Calla asked, giving him a crooked smile.

Yeah, the door, Raoul replied.

It'll be fine, I assured him. *We'll make it on time.*

Not if she continues to move at this glacial pace. Armageddon has a better chance of happening first.

I patted Calla's hand. "I'm sorry about your fight with Ruby. I think if you tell her the truth, she'll understand."

"I felt so embarrassed," Calla admitted.

"If you have a spell to fix the problem, then you can wear the necklace the next time you see her," Marley added. "Show her that you cared enough to address the problem."

Calla pressed her hand against her heart. "I'm so glad I came here. You two are better than a druid healer." She scanned the small pots on the table. "Now, which plants can I teach you about today?"

Marley pointed to the one on the far left. "We're learning about living stone plants at school. I wouldn't mind earning extra credit."

Calla chuckled. "There's that butt-kissing spirit I admire. I'd be more than happy to share a few lesser-known details about this one."

"What's a living stone plant?" I asked.

"That's the spirit, Ember," Calla said. "Never be afraid to show your ignorance."

"They're small succulents with an invisible root system," Marley told me.

"They blend into their surroundings incredibly well," Calla added. "So well, in fact, that it's almost impossible to notice them."

Marley's shoulders straightened as she prepared to absorb whatever wisdom Calla imparted. She was my little knowledge sponge, whereas I was just a wet sponge—heavier than I should be and ineffective at cleaning.

I half listened as Calla droned on about the characteristics of the plant. Raoul yawned. Even PP3 trotted into the kitchen, did a semicircle, and trotted straight back to the sofa. Wise dog.

My gaze flicked to the clock. "Sheriff Nash will be here soon," I said. I hadn't intended to say the words aloud, but out they tumbled.

"Oh, are you two together again?" Calla asked.

She'd either forgotten or hadn't heard an update in quite some time.

"They're going to get married," Marley interjected, smiling broadly.

Calla drew back. "You're engaged?"

"Not yet," I said, "but the right noises are being made."

"He already told Aunt Hyacinth," Marley said.

This time I glared at her. I didn't want everyone to know our personal business. The news would spread through the coven like wildfire.

What are you worried about? Raoul asked. *Calla will forget the moment she leaves the cottage.*

Good point.

"You deserve every happiness," Calla told me. "You've endured so much grief and disappointment for a witch your age." She shook her head. "It's time for a change of luck."

"Amen to that," I said.

Calla leaned over the small pot on the right. "Oh, look at that. Your plant has taken a bad turn."

Frowning, Marley leaned over to inspect the plant. "I hadn't even noticed. Is it dead?"

Calla touched the leaf with a delicate finger, and it snapped off. "I think so."

"I've been studying so much lately," Marley lamented. "I must've missed this one during my rounds. Is there anything we can do?"

"Compost heap?" I suggested.

Both witches turned to glower at me.

"What?" I asked innocently. "It's a plant. Circle of life and all that."

"It's a living thing," Marley countered. "Show some respect."

"*Was* a living thing." I flicked the plant, causing another crunchy leaf to fall.

"Such a pity," Calla said.

"Is there a way to revive it?" I asked. The question surprised even me; the idea seemed to sprout from nowhere.

"You mean bring it back from the dead?" Calla pondered the plant. "Yes, I do believe there is."

Marley perked up. "Really?"

"The spell wouldn't work on anything bigger than a plant, mind you, but it should work for this little fella." Calla looked at Marley. "May I see your books, duckling?"

Marley raced from the kitchen and returned with a stack of spell books. "Is this dangerous?" she asked, not sounding the least bit worried—and yet she was terrified of a Ferris wheel.

"Not in such a small dose," Calla told her. "You'd never want to attempt anything beyond this though. That would invite unforeseen consequences."

"The call is coming from inside the house," I said in my best horror-movie voice.

Ignoring me, Calla flipped through the books until she located the spell she wanted. "Here we are."

Marley leaned over her shoulder to review the spell. "It looks fairly simple."

Calla chuckled. "Only because you're so advanced for your age."

I glanced at the clock again. "How long will this spell take?" And would it work on us after Aunt Hyacinth killed us for tardiness?

"In Marley's capable hands, not long at all," Calla said.

I forced a smile at my daughter. "No pressure, Marley. Tick tock."

She understood. My whip-smart kid crafted a potion in under two minutes and poured the foul-smelling mixture into the soil. Calla acted as an observer, only commenting once on the amount of crushed daffodils Marley had added to the concoction. Marley double-checked her measurement and made the adjustment. I felt a deep sense of pride watching my daughter master a complex task. This was much more interesting than watching her color inside the lines when she was younger.

Color and moisture returned to the plant. "This is incredible, Calla," Marley said, stroking the regenerated leaf. "Thank you so much for the lesson."

"Happy to help," Calla replied. "You know, with talent like yours, you should spend time at the senior citizens home. I bet there are plenty of old folks that could use a bit of magical assistance with everyday tasks like clasps and shoelaces."

"A magical candy striper," I said. "That would be great volunteer work for you, Marley."

Her blue eyes brightened. "It would. I love that idea. Thanks, Calla."

"I should be going now," Calla said, slowly rising to her feet. As much as I enjoyed the older witch's company, it took all my strength not to show my relief. Punctuality was more important than pleasure right now.

"Here, let me help you," I said. I offered an arm to assist her to the front door.

Calla hooked her arm through mine. "Such strength," she remarked, patting me gently. "Must be the Rose in you."

The knots in my stomach loosened the moment I opened the front door. "Must be."

Chapter Two

Now that Sheriff Granger Nash had a couple Sunday dinners under his utility belt, he seemed to understand the assignment. Look presentable. Compliment the hostess. Eat the food. Compliment the hostess. And so on. Which made his current decision all the more surprising.

I stared at the cowboy hat that darkened my doorstep, completely ignoring the man underneath it. Thanks to Calla's unexpected visit, there was no time for a fashion emergency.

"Raccoon got your tongue?" the hat asked.

"You can't wear that to dinner."

Granger's grin stretched to the sides of his face. "What's the worst that can happen?"

"Have you met my aunt?"

Marley appeared beside me for a glimpse of the monstrosity in question. "I like it. It adds character."

"It adds fear and loathing to what is already a stressful meal," I argued.

Granger chuckled. "What's stressful about it? We've

got it down to a science now." He hooked his thumbs through his belt loops. "Ready to go? Your carriage awaits."

"Is it an actual horse and buggy?" Given his attire, it wouldn't surprise me.

"I think Hyacinth will find it charming."

"You overestimate her willingness to be charmed by Western couture."

Marley gave me a tiny shove across the threshold. "Let's go," she said. "We don't want to be late."

PP3 barked.

"Don't worry," I told the Yorkshire terrier. "I'll bring you a doggy bag."

He lowered his head to the cushion, satisfied.

I watched with amusement as Granger tried to duck behind the wheel without dislodging his hat. He gave me an awkward smile as he tried again.

"You're having the opposite problem of Bolan," I said, sliding easily into the passenger seat. The leprechaun needed a booster seat to see over the steering wheel.

Marley sat alone in the back. "We could've walked. The house is right there." She waved a hand between the front seats in the direction of Thornhold, the massive family estate where my aunt resided, along with her staff. My cousin Florian lived in a man cave in what passed for a basement in the sprawling mansion.

"If we traipsed through the house in muddy shoes, Aunt Hyacinth would catch a case of the vapors."

"What does she care?" Marley asked. "It isn't like she's the one who cleans."

"No, but she's the one who has exacting standards that she expects others to abide by."

As Granger drove away from Rose Cottage, I noticed

the uncomfortable slump of his shoulders. "You're being impressively stubborn right now," I said.

He gazed straight ahead. "It is impressive, isn't it?"

"You can't turn to look at me, can you?"

"Of course not. I need to keep my eyes on the road."

"Yes, the very busy road that connects the cottage to Thornhold. Take off the hat and admit defeat."

"Never."

He parked in front of the mansion and extricated himself from the car without knocking off the hat.

"Someone's been practicing," I remarked as we strode toward the front door.

"I like your boots," Marley told him. "They add extra flair."

"Yes, if anything speaks to Aunt Hyacinth, it's flair." My sarcasm wasn't lost on Granger.

He squeezed my hand. "You're overthinking it. She's come a long way."

"All the more reason not to set her back a few squares."

The door opened, and we were greeted by Simon, my mother's right hand. And left hand. Basically, he performed all the tasks my aunt considered beneath her. Unsurprisingly, his gaze went directly to the hat.

"Good evening," Simon said, seemingly to the hat. "I see you've brought a friend. I'll have to set an extra plate."

Granger patted the hat. "He's just here for the excellent company."

"Miss Linnea and her family won't be with us tonight, I'm afraid," Simon informed us. "It seems Master Hudson is playing in a sports tournament this weekend."

"Is the lady of the house not taking it well?" I asked.

"She resisted the urge to call the athletic director and demand that games no longer be held on Sundays."

"I'm proud of her restraint." Although I could understand the desire to keep at least one day of the week free from obligations. Kids needed time to recharge as much as adults did.

The rest of my family were already seated at the table, except my aunt. Florian sat beside Aster. On her other side was Ackley. Her husband, Sterling, sat opposite her, beside the other twin, Aspen. Their plan seemed to be divide and conquer the table.

I took my usual seat next to Florian. Marley sat beside Sterling and left the chair across from me free for Granger. He didn't love sitting adjacent to my aunt, but he tolerated the close proximity in exchange for proximity to me.

Aunt Hyacinth breezed into the room, carrying a half-filled cocktail. She wore one of her statement kaftans; this one was covered in brightly colored llamas wearing floral necklaces. I decided not to ask.

The moment she took her place at the head of the table, her gaze snagged on the hat. "How fetching, Sheriff. Did you have it imported from deep in the heart of Texas?"

"No, deep in the heart of my closet. It's been there for a long time. Belonged to my father. I decided to dust it off and give it a second chance at life."

I felt a momentary pang of guilt for mocking the hat. The death of Granger's father had been the worst time of his life. Naturally, the hat would have sentimental value.

"That's very sweet." Aunt Hyacinth's gaze swung toward Florian and Aster. "Do you think you might wear one of my kaftans someday out of love and respect for your dearly departed mother?"

Florian started to choke and set down his pint of beer.

"Aster would look captivating in any one of them," Sterling interjected. Marley could learn a few butt-kissing tricks from the wizard.

"I'd like the flamingo one," Aster said.

"You hate the flamingo one," Ackley chimed in. "You said it looks like bloodstains that somebody tried to remove with bleach."

Aster covered her son's hand and squeezed. Hard. "No, sweetheart. You're thinking of something else."

"What else looks like it's covered in bloodstains?" Ackley pressed.

Your face if you keep this up, I thought to myself.

"Why don't we change the conversation to a more palatable topic?" my aunt suggested.

Talk about personal growth.

"What's on the menu tonight, Aunt Hyacinth?" Marley asked. Her anxiety was often soothed by knowing what to expect, and that included dinner options.

"Filet mignon," Simon said from the doorway.

On cue, platters and plates floated from the kitchen to the table. It didn't quite rise to the level of *Be Our Guest*, but the parade was always enjoyable to watch. One of the plates skimmed Granger's hat. He lowered his head until the threat had passed.

"Before we begin, why don't we go around the table and each say something we're grateful for?" Aunt Hyacinth said.

Silence followed the suggestion.

"No one?" my aunt finally asked. "Fine. I'll start."

"It isn't that we have nothing to be grateful for," Florian began. "It's only that we weren't expecting to be put on the spot."

She looked down her nose at him, which was impressive given her shorter stature. "Is it so challenging that you need time to prepare?"

"I'm grateful for my mom," Marley piped up. "She's the best."

"The best what?" my aunt prompted.

"The best at understanding me, probably because we're so much alike."

I choked on my water. "Alike?" Marley was light-years ahead of me in terms of ... well, everything.

"I'm grateful that I'm invited to Sunday dinners," Granger said, cutting his meat with restraint. The werewolf inside him probably wanted to devour it whole.

"I'm grateful that Hudson isn't here," Ackley said. "He always pinches food off my plate."

"I'm grateful for beer," Florian said, tipping back his glass and draining it dry.

"I have the utmost gratitude for Sidhe Shed," Aster said. "I never dreamed it would be successful so quickly."

Sterling smiled at her. "I had faith in you, darling. You're a force to be reckoned with."

"Like mother, like daughter," my aunt said with a prim smile.

"I'm grateful that Ackley stopped wetting the bed," Aspen interjected.

"What does it matter to you?" Aster asked. "You two don't share a bed."

"No, but he's the top bunk," Aspen replied. "It was like living under a faucet."

Ackley threw a buttered roll across the table, prompting Aspen to hold up his plate as a shield. Unfortunately, the plate had been filled with food.

"Well, this little experiment went well," Aunt Hyacinth said wryly.

There was a sudden snapping sound, and my ears began to ring. Other noises were muffled to the point where I felt like I was underwater. I closed my eyes as though that would help. Once the sound returned to normal, I opened my eyes again. A wolf in a cowboy hat stared back at me.

"Granger?"

The wolf howled.

"Sweet baby Elvis," I said under my breath. It wasn't just Granger that had transformed. It was everybody at the table. In place of Marley was a younger version of me. Sterling looked like a child playing dress-up in adult clothes. In Aspen's chair sat a small yet adorable monster with bulging eyes and a long tongue hanging out of his mouth.

I turned to regard Florian, who looked exactly the same. Aster was similar to her usual godly appearance, except with a more professional hue. She wore wire-rimmed glasses, and her white-blond hair was swept up in a respectable bun. Her cardigan set had morphed into a business suit.

"What's going on with all of you?" Florian asked, aghast.

Aunt Hyacinth shimmered like a celestial being.

"Are your boobs bigger?" I asked.

My aunt dropped her gaze to her chest. "They seem the same to me, and I'll thank you for not discussing my body parts. It's poor manners, especially at the dinner table."

I turned toward Florian. "How do I look?" I asked, almost afraid to know the answer.

Florian's gaze flicked over me. "Just the teeniest, tiniest bit older."

"Am I going to look in the mirror and see old Rose from *Titanic*?"

"No, not at all. I'm serious. You look mostly the same."

"Did somebody do magic at the table?" Sterling demanded, although his voice squeaked like a child's.

A phone trilled, and I realized it was Granger's. The wolf used his snout to nudge the phone across the table toward me. I leaned over and swiped it from the table.

"It's Deputy Bolan," I said, reading the screen.

The wolf nodded as in, "Answer it."

"What's up, Bolan?" I asked, trying to maintain a casual air. No reason to freak out the leprechaun by telling him about his boss's current condition.

"Where's the sheriff?"

"Indisposed at the moment. He told me to answer the call."

"You guys changed, too, didn't you?"

"Changed how?" I asked, a tad too cheery.

"I don't know. Something strange happened. I was having dinner with my husband when everybody ... changed. Then somebody dropped dead right in the middle of the restaurant."

"Dropped dead from the spell?"

"No idea yet. I wanted Sheriff Nash to assess the situation."

I looked at the sheriff. He wasn't in any position to respond to a call like that. "Where are you?"

"Whistlin' Pixie."

"Oh, that new place. How is it?"

"It was great, until the spell hit, and somebody died. I recommend the hush puppies though."

Yum. I loved hush puppies. "I'll meet you there in ten minutes."

Bolan groaned. "I don't want you, Rose. I want the sheriff."

"Well, you can't always get what you want," I told the ungrateful leprechaun. "You get what you need."

"It might've been a heart attack," he said slowly. "You stay put. I can handle it."

"If you really believe that, you wouldn't be calling the sheriff. See you in ten minutes." I hung up.

"What's going on?" my aunt asked.

I rose to my feet. "Emergency. I need to help."

The wolf attempted to follow me. "Down, boy," I said. Between a wide-reaching spell and a sudden death, we couldn't let residents know that the sheriff was trapped as a wolf. It might set off mass hysteria.

"Is there anything I can do?" Aster asked.

"Make sure Marley eats her vegetables." I hurried from the mansion. It was only when I arrived outside that I realized I'd have to drive the sheriff's car. I heard a noise behind me and saw the wolf had disregarded my command.

"Some K-9 unit you are." I opened the passenger door, and he jumped inside. "You have to stay in the car. I promise I'll report everything to you."

The wolf howled in protest.

"Fine, but at least take off the hat." I removed the hat and set it neatly on the seat behind him. "Not because I hate it, I swear. I don't want it to get ruined." Which it most certainly would if he continued to wear it in his wolf form.

The wolf licked my hand in gratitude.

I drove toward the restaurant, wondering what kind of spell had been cast and, more importantly, how on earth we'd undo it.

Chapter Three

Whistlin' Pixie was nearly deserted by the time I arrived. It seemed the spell had caused most patrons to flee, hopefully not without paying their bills first.

"No dogs allowed," the host said from behind the stand.

Wolf Granger growled in response. The host held up his hands in acquiescence and let us inside.

"Where's the deputy?" I asked.

With his gaze still locked on the wolf, the host pointed to a private area at the back of the restaurant.

I didn't recognize the supernatural that met us there. He was tall and buff, with the kind of copper-toned skin that suggested a lifetime enjoying the rays of a blazing sun. "I'm looking for Deputy Bolan. He should be here."

"It's me, Rose," he said. "I'm Bolan."

My eyes nearly bugged out of my head. "How?"

He shrugged a pair of ridiculously broad shoulders. "Ask the spell." The former leprechaun didn't seem surprised to see the wolf loping beside me. "I knew he wouldn't obey orders."

I stared at the new deputy like the host stared at the wolf.

"You might want to close your mouth before you catch a fly. I'm pretty sure I saw somebody turn into one," Bolan said.

I clamped my mouth closed. "You won't need to sit on phone books to see over the steering wheel anymore."

"Not really on my mind at the moment. I did mention the dead guy, right?"

Who could think about a dead guy at a time like this? I was far more interested in figuring out why Bolan looked like a backup dancer for Magic Mike.

Granger got me back on track. The wolf had sniffed out the corpse on the other side of the table and was already examining the surrounding area.

"I guess the spell turned him into his wolf form," Bolan said.

"Thank you for your service, Deputy Obvious. Do we know if all shifters reverted to their animal states?"

"No. There was a wereferret in here that I know. He changed, but not into a ferret—into a giant rat."

I shuddered. Rodents were not my thing. Giant rats even less so.

"Have you identified the deceased?" I asked.

"His name is Bertram Lapp. Seventy years old today. That's why they were here celebrating. Widowed."

I glanced around the empty room. "Who else was celebrating?"

"I sequestered them in the kitchen so I could section off this area."

"You seem determined to make this a crime," I said.

"No, the marks on the victim's neck make this a potential crime."

I eyed an uneaten flatbread on the table, smothered in multiple cheeses and prosciutto. "I'll tell you what's a crime. That abandoned meal right there."

"They can get a doggy bag," Bolan said. He cast a guilty look in the sheriff's direction. "No offense."

I walked over to study the body. White hair. Delicate features. A kind face. Then again, every lifeless face seemed kind when there was no subconscious driving the expressions.

Bolan motioned to the table, where a row of empty tumblers was clustered at the head of the table. "I suspect he was deep in his cups when the spell hit."

"A drink for each year of his life?" I suggested wryly. "Any chance Bertram cast the spell and died from the intensity?" He could've left marks by clutching his own neck if he'd been struggling to breathe.

"Doubtful," Bolan replied. "He was a fairy."

I shot him a quizzical look. "Fairies have magic."

"Not like this."

I glanced at the corpse. "He doesn't look like a fairy now. Where are his wings?"

"Maybe the spell got rid of them."

"I guess the other members of his party can tell us." I turned to the wolf. "Granger, stay."

The wolf's eyes turned to amber slits.

Bolan and I walked to the kitchen where only one paranormal awaited us.

"I counted more place settings than two," I said.

"They were too freaked out to stay," the middle-aged fairy volunteered. His wings were small but intact. His eyes burned like two active volcanoes. Other than that, his appearance seemed relatively normal.

"Do your eyes always look like that?" I asked. I was torn

between my interest in the spell and the dead body in the other room.

He gave me a blank look, so I spun him toward the shiny refrigerator. His red eyes rounded at his reflection.

"Now that's what I call bloodshot," he said. "Can't say I'm surprised. Between planning this party and my hectic work schedule, I've been short on sleep."

"You planned this party for Bertram?"

"Yes. He's my father. I'm Jeremiah Lapp."

"Ember Rose."

He shook my hand. "My brother was around here somewhere, but I think he took off along with everybody else."

I cocked an eyebrow. "He took off?"

"He has a hard time staying still. He tends to wander when he gets bored."

"I'm sorry. His father just dropped dead, and he left because he was bored?"

Jeremiah seemed to realize his mistake. "Poor choice of words. Timothy's a pacer. He takes a potion to calm his nerves, but I think this evening's events were too overwhelming."

Fair enough.

I turned to see Bolan behind me. "Where'd you go?"

"I was checking to see whether anybody was waiting in the dining area."

"Was Timothy Lapp there, by any chance?" I asked.

Bolan shook his head as he scribbled down notes. "Nobody except staff."

My gaze swung back to Jeremiah. "Any idea where your brother might've gone?"

Jeremiah rubbed his forehead. "Home? The woods near Stonewall Park? Who knows with Timothy? He tends to do the unexpected."

"I'll worry about him later," Bolan said. "Mr. Lapp, I'd like a complete list of everybody who attended the dinner."

Jeremiah blinked at him. "Why does it matter?"

"We'll need to speak with them," the deputy explained.

"What do you think happened to him?" Jeremiah asked.

"We were hoping you could tell us," Bolan said.

"It happened so suddenly. One minute he was seated at the table and the next minute…" He frowned. "I don't know. Everything was a blur. He'd had an asthma attack earlier, but he seemed fine during dinner."

"How much earlier?" Bolan asked.

"When he got here. The party was a surprise." Jeremiah grimaced. "In hindsight, I think that was a bad idea. The surprise stressed him out, and stress triggers his asthma."

"Did you see him fall to the floor?" I asked.

"No. Once the spell hit, it was too chaotic to focus on anything. There was screaming and crashing dishes." He shuddered at the memory.

"It did get crazy for a few minutes," Bolan agreed. "The giant rat sent everyone running in the main dining area."

"Totally understandable," I murmured.

"How many of you were in the room when he died?" Bolan asked.

"I don't know," Jeremiah said. "Some fled the room and returned when they saw the chaos in the dining room. Some didn't come back." He wiped tears from his cheek. "I found my dad on the floor and yelled for help. To be honest, I can't even remember who was there at that point."

"Does your father normally have wings?" I asked.

Jeremiah jerked to attention. "Yes. Why?"

"Because he doesn't have them now," I said.

"I was so shaken up; I hadn't even noticed." Jeremiah

looked at the deputy. "Do you think somebody targeted my father with that spell?"

Bolan grunted. "A spell that seems to have affected the whole town? That's pretty far fetched. We'll know more once we get the preliminary report. I can share the information with you then."

"You're certain he's dead?" Jeremiah asked. "Is there a chance he just got knocked unconscious from the spell?"

"I'm sorry, Mr. Lapp," Bolan said. "I confirmed it myself."

Jeremiah nodded slowly. "I can give you the list of guests. I have all their contact details." His voice was devoid of emotion at this point. Jeremiah Lapp seemed well and truly spent.

"I'm sorry about your father, Mr. Lapp," I said. I still remembered losing my dad like it happened yesterday. The pain never left me; it simply got absorbed by my bloodstream and circulated throughout my body so that it lessened in intensity over time. Or so I told myself.

"Thank you. This will take time to process." Jeremiah's wings fluttered. "What about the spell? Do we know when it will end?"

"We don't even know what the spell is yet," Bolan said. He looked at me. "We're going to have a very busy week."

Jeremiah unbuttoned the top couple buttons of his shirt. "I'd like to pay the bill now, if possible. Then I'd like to go home and make arrangements for my father. And here I thought I was all finished planning parties for the foreseeable future."

"Not much of a party," I said.

"My father would want it that way. It was the same when my mother died. He insisted on a celebration of life."

I could see the appeal, although a selfish part of me

would like a bunch of wailing mourners at my funeral, too grief-stricken to enjoy alcohol or cake. Maybe someone could even drop to their knees, shake a fist at the universe, and scream, "Why?" I wisely kept the thought to myself.

"Where's Thomas?" I asked, once Jeremiah left and we returned to the private area with Bertram Lapp.

"He went home as soon as we heard about the death. He knew I'd need to work."

"I'm sorry your dinner got interrupted."

"Death waits for no meal."

"Very profound. Do you really think there's foul play involved?"

"I can't ignore the marks on his neck."

I thought of Calla and her trouble with the necklace. "Maybe he had trouble with a tie while he was getting dressed for dinner."

"Or maybe he likes it rough." Bolan shrugged. "We'll wait for a professional to weigh in, but my gut says murder."

Wolf Granger trotted over to join us and licked my hand. "Granger agrees with you." I scratched behind his ear.

"Don't worry, Sheriff," Bolan said. "We've got this under control."

The wolf started to lick the deputy's hand, then seemed to think better of it.

"Well, at least this was a night to remember," I said.

Bolan gazed in the direction of the private room. "Unfortunately, I think it's one they'd rather forget."

I awoke the next day, thinking the spell might've broken overnight. No such luck. Mini Me went to school, and I spotted the same wrinkles on my face that had appeared during dinner.

No one had seen Linnea since the spell took hold, so I decided to drop by Palmetto House and check on her. Although she'd sent a group text to say she and the kids were fine, it would be typical of Linnea to be trapped under a refrigerator at the time she wrote it.

The house was eerily quiet. No Bryn or Hudson. Presumably, they'd left for school, which was a good sign. On the other hand, there was no sign of guests at the inn, which *wasn't* such a good sign.

"Linnea?" I walked through the historic house in search of my cousin. Other than the absence of guests, nothing seemed amiss. "Hello?"

I passed through the dining room and into the kitchen. "Linnea, are you home?"

"I'm here," a voice squeaked.

"Where?" I scanned the kitchen for my statuesque cousin. The top of a white-blond head popped above the countertops and quickly disappeared. Peering over the edge, I saw a tiny Linnea jumping up to be seen.

"Down here," she said, waving.

"You said you were fine!"

"I *am* fine. I'm a leprechaun without the green," she squeaked again. "No big deal."

"Only a small one." The spell had turned Sterling into a child, yet Linnea seemed to be smaller than the size of one. It made no sense.

"I had to cancel all the reservations this week," she said. "I can't function like this." She spread her tiny arms wide.

"Maybe not, but you're freakin' adorable." I scooped her up and set her on the counter. "What about the kids?"

"Hudson has more muscle and looks like Wyatt.

Bryn looks the same to me, although she claims to have a mustache and a zit on her chin. I couldn't see them."

"To be fair, it's probably hard to see anything from that distance."

Linnea scowled.

"What about Rick?" Linnea's boyfriend was a minotaur. I was half hoping he'd shrunk to her size; they'd make an adorable set.

"Unchanged. I don't know why he'd be unaffected by the spell. He was with us at Hudson's game when it hit."

"Florian wasn't affected either. What about others at the game?"

Linnea swung her tiny legs back and forth. "It was pandemonium. Rick put me in his pocket and grabbed the kids so we could hightail it out of there."

"What about Wyatt?"

She snorted. "You think he actually made good on a promise and showed up for the tournament? I have no idea. Haven't heard from him."

I wondered whether he'd turned into a wolf like his brother. "Would you mind calling to see if he answers?"

Linnea scoffed. "Why would I do a thing like that? The phone works both ways."

"Granger is a wolf. I'm wondering if the spell impacted Wyatt the same way."

"Would serve him right." She paused. "Although I'm sorry for Granger." She pointed to the opposite end of the counter. "Pass me the phone, please. I don't want to throw my back out trying to lift it."

"I'll make the call. You do the talking." I retrieved the phone and hit the button for Wyatt, who was listed in her contacts as 'Good for Nothing.'

Wyatt's sleepy voice answered the call. "What do you need now, Linnea?"

She looked affronted. "Nothing from you," she chirped. "Ember wants to know how you were affected by the spell."

"What spell?"

It seemed Wyatt had escaped the effects as well.

"Nothing out of the ordinary happened to you last night?" I asked.

"Nope."

"Then why did you miss Hudson's game?" Linnea demanded.

"Oh, that was yesterday? I thought it was next week." The lie rolled effortlessly off his tongue.

"If you'd shown up, you'd know there's been a spell that has somehow affected most of the town."

"Your brother is stuck in his wolf form," I said. "You might want to check on your mom."

"You're serious? Everybody's been affected?"

"A lot of residents, although not all," I said.

Wyatt chuckled.

"I'm glad you find this amusing," Linnea ranted.

"You sound like you're calling me from the inside of a tin cup," Wyatt told her. "What did the spell do to you?"

Linnea shook her head at me. "Nothing," she lied. "And your kids are fine, too, thanks for asking."

"I know you wouldn't let anything happen to them," Wyatt said. "You're a good mom."

Linnea stared at the phone. "Are you sure the spell didn't get you?"

"Don't make me regret saying something nice," Wyatt replied. "Any idea which member of your coven is responsible for this mess?"

Linnea folded her arms in a huff. "What makes you

think anyone in our coven would cast a spell over all of Starry Hollow?"

"Because it's exactly the level of arrogance I'd expect from your kind."

Aaaand Wyatt was back.

Linnea's little face scrunched in dismay. I shook my head at her. Wyatt was pushing her buttons. There was no point in indulging him.

"Ember's right," Linnea said. "You should check on your mother." She disconnected the call. "Typical. He skates through another disaster. Can you believe he didn't ask about the kids? What if they were wolves too?"

"He'll never change, Linnea," I said, not even when there was a spell that changed everybody else, apparently.

"I don't suppose you know what caused this?" Linnea asked.

"Not yet, but I'm working on it with Granger's office. He's obviously out of commission."

"I hope it breaks soon because I can't live like this."

"Is there anything I can do for you while I'm here? I'm happy to help."

Linnea stared longingly at the refrigerator. "I'm hungry. Would you mind opening the fridge door and getting me something to eat?"

"Of course." I opened the fridge and scouted for appropriate options. "What about your wand?"

"I can't reach it. I'd been keeping it under my bed, but I moved it to the top shelf of my closet last week when I was vacuuming."

I opened a packet of cheese. "I can get that for you, too, before I leave."

"You're a hero."

I prepared a meal of tiny portions and hurried to

Linnea's bedroom to retrieve her wand. "If there's anything else, please call me. If I can't help for some reason, I'll send Marley or someone else who can."

"Once the kids are home from school, I'll be okay. And Rick will be here after work."

"If you're sure…"

"You go ahead, Ember. I'm sure there are plenty of paranormals worse off than I am."

"You can say that again. One of them's dead."

Linnea glanced around the room. "There's something to be said for a different vantage point. I can see dust particles I've missed."

"I'm not sure that's a bright side."

I left Linnea to her scrutiny. As I stepped into the sunshine, my phone buzzed in my pocket. I pulled it out to see Deputy Bolan's name on the screen. "Any news?" I asked, not bothering to exchange pleasantries.

"Got the preliminary report on Bertram Lapp," Bolan said.

"That was fast."

"I may have expressed impatience."

"I'm surprised that worked," I said. Bolan's impatience generally consisted of a well-placed huff.

"I may have expressed impatience by standing over him all night until he completed the examination."

"Wow. You're really leaning into this whole buff Bolan thing."

He ignored the remark. "It was definitely murder."

"How did he die?"

"Painfully."

"Very scientific."

"I was right about the marks on his neck. They were thumb-shaped bruises. Bertram Lapp was strangled."

"Is it possible he was choking on food and made those marks himself?"

"There was nothing obstructing his airway from the inside, only the outside."

"What about the asthma attack?" I asked. "Could it have been another one?"

"Rose, are you choosing to ignore the marks on his neck consistent with strangulation?"

"No, but how could the fairy have been brutally murdered in public and no one noticed?"

"Under normal circumstances, I'd agree with you, but I know what the restaurant was like at the time. It was pandemonium. And the asthma attack Lapp had at the start of dinner didn't do him any favors."

"What do you mean?"

"Typically, strangulation might take four or five minutes, but because the victim was older and still deprived of oxygen from the asthma attack, he died faster than he might've otherwise. Made the killer's job easier."

"Did the spell do anything to him aside from remove his wings?" I asked, thinking of my fine lines and wrinkles. "Maybe it made him older and more fragile."

"Could be. I'll see if we can piece that together from his medical history."

"We need to speak to the other son," I said.

"Already on it. The sheriff tracked his scent to the woods. Pitt's on traffic duty, so I figured I'd ask you to meet me there."

I smiled at the phone. "Granger insisted, didn't he?"

"His growl is very persuasive," Bolan admitted.

"I'm at Palmetto House now. Give me the location, and I'll see you there in a few minutes."

Chapter Four

Timothy Lapp wasn't at his house. Bolan and I eventually found him in the backyard of his father's house, which was the house he and Jeremiah had grown up in.

Bolan glanced up at the large treehouse in the backyard. "Is he twelve?"

"Maybe he is. Who knows what the spell did to him? If you can grow taller and less green, there's no reason why Timothy Lapp can't grow shorter and less mature."

Without knowing the details of the spell, it was impossible to know what to expect.

"There's no ladder," Bolan complained.

"Fairy, remember?" It seemed that the spell had allowed Timothy to keep his wings. "After you, Deputy." I made a sweeping gesture.

He gave me a long look. "Are you afraid of heights, Rose?"

"No, I'm afraid of pulling a muscle. Pull-ups were not one of my strengths in gym class."

"Did you have any strengths in gym class?"

"Ouch, did that spell make your attitude bigger too?"

Buff Bolan climbed the branches with ease and reached the top of the treehouse.

"To the monkey manor born," I quipped. The leprechaun-sized deputy wouldn't have been able to do that. He would've waited for me at the base of the tree or asked me to conjure a spell to give him a boost.

Right, a spell. The idea should've occurred to me sooner. I rummaged around in my oversized purse until I located my wand.

"*Elevatus*," I said. My body rose in the air until I was level with the opening to the treehouse.

Timothy sat on the floor with his arms wrapped around his shins. Bright green wings were tucked together behind him.

Bolan craned his neck to regard me. "He's not saying anything."

I lowered myself to the floor of the treehouse. "Hey, Timothy. My name is Ember, and this is Deputy Bolan. Mind if we talk to you?"

Timothy didn't look at us.

"I'm sorry about your father," I continued. "I'm sure you must be in shock."

"Of course I'm in shock!" he blurted. "He was my dad. How could he drop dead like that in the middle of his own birthday party?" Tears streamed down his cheeks. "The universe has a cruel sense of humor."

"Your father had help, Mr. Lapp," Bolan said. "That's what we'd like to discuss with you."

"Help?" Timothy's brow creased in confusion. "You mean his asthma?"

Bolan shook his head. "Not his asthma."

"You mean someone killed him?" He paused, digesting the news. "How? There would've been a dozen witnesses."

"And yet no one saw anything," I said.

Timothy wore a pained expression. "What kind of monster would do such a thing?"

"We were hoping you could tell us," I said.

Timothy rested his chin between his knees. "I don't know. I was in the bathroom when the spell hit."

"How convenient," Bolan said.

"It's the truth," Timothy shot back.

"You have to admit," I said, "it's pretty suspicious that you happened to be in the restroom at the exact moment the spell hit, and your father died."

Timothy's gaze dropped to the floor. "I guess I can see that."

"Your father was strangled," Bolan offered.

Timothy gave us a blank look.

"Oftentimes that kind of violence is personal," Bolan continued, "which makes sense given it happened while he was surrounded by friends and family."

"You seriously think one of us would do that to him?" Timothy shook his head. "Everybody loved my dad."

"The fact is that somebody *did* do that to him," I said.

"What can you tell us about the dinner party?" Bolan asked. "Anything stand out to you? Any disagreements?"

"Last night was such a mess," Timothy said. "Even before the spell hit, there was a lot happening. My dad freaked out about the surprise and that set off his asthma. My brother invited too many guests, and we had to add place settings."

"Why too many?" I asked.

"Because he knows I don't like a crowd."

"But it was a party for your father, not you," Bolan pointed out.

"Doesn't matter. Any time Jeremiah can annoy me, he goes for it." His gaze skated from Bolan to me. "Either one of you got a brother?"

"No," we said in unison.

Timothy grunted. "Zero stars. Do not recommend."

"Why not help Jeremiah plan the party?" I suggested. "That would've made it difficult to annoy you with the decisions he made."

"Oh, please. And deny Jeremiah sole credit for the occasion?" Timothy blew a raspberry. "Fat chance of that ever happening."

"Was there anybody present who might've had a grudge against your dad?" I asked. "Someone who seized the opportunity during the chaos of the spell to even the score?"

"Not that I know of. My father and I weren't super close though."

"Any reason why not?" Bolan asked.

"Are you close to your father?" Timothy shot back, slightly defensive.

"Mine's dead," I said.

"My relationship is strained," Bolan said.

"You're the black sheep too, huh?" Timothy asked.

"No, I'm the gay sheep," Bolan answered smoothly.

In all the time I'd known him, I didn't recall the leprechaun talking about his parents. I felt mildly guilty that I didn't know about his estranged relationship with his father.

"At least you joined a respected profession and made something of yourself," Timothy said. "My old man was still waiting for me to be less of an embarrassment. Time ran out, I guess."

"How did the spell affect you, Timothy?" I asked.

"My wings are a duller shade of green, according to my roommate. They look the same to me. And he said my face looks like it's got this perpetual hangdog expression."

"That's it?" Bolan asked.

Timothy nodded. "As far as I know."

"What about the rest of the party?" I asked.

"You think I noticed them when there was a giant rat running around? I felt sick to my stomach during the meal, which is why I went to the bathroom. I heard shouting, and by the time I got back to the room, my dad was dead on the floor." He broke off, appearing to collect himself.

"And you decided not to stick around," I pointed out.

"I couldn't stay there. It was all too much. I wasn't the best son. I always thought I'd have time to redeem myself before he died. Fairies have long life spans for that sort of thing."

"Only if nobody decides to kill them before then," Bolan countered.

"Would you describe your father as fit and healthy?" I asked.

"Aside from the asthma, sure, although he wouldn't have agreed. He was always saying how frail he felt on the inside. He was convinced he'd die before my mom, but obviously, that didn't happen." Tears glistened in his eyes. "Who would want to kill my dad? He was the kind of man who looked out for everybody. That's why my brother had to invite so many randos to the party."

"Would you say he looked out for you?" I asked gently.

"I guess, but I know deep down he wished I was more like Jeremiah and Tyler."

"Who's Tyler?" I asked.

Bolan answered for him. "Tyler Adams worked with the

victim. Some kind of underling. He's on the guest list."

"Any animosity between your dad and Tyler?" I asked.

"Definitely not," Timothy replied. "My father spoke highly of him. Dad treated him like another son."

"That must've been hard for you, given your own complicated relationship with him," I said.

Timothy pinned me with a hard stare. "Are we finished now? I'd like to get back to my brooding. I feel a few song lyrics coming on."

"If you think of anything, please let us know," Bolan said. "In the meantime, don't leave town."

Timothy frowned. "I'm scheduled to play a gig an hour away this weekend."

"Unless we solve the case by then, the fans will have to be disappointed," Bolan said, as he began his descent from the treehouse. I followed behind him. It was easier for me to climb down without magic.

"Life is so unfair," Timothy said.

Bolan tilted his head back to regard the treehouse. "I think your father would agree."

I returned to the cottage, still ruminating on the conversation with Timothy. I only made it a few steps into the living room when I stopped short at the sight of PP3 on the sofa, wearing a pair of sunglasses and a black North Face puffer jacket.

"Marley," I called.

She's upstairs. Raoul wandered in from the kitchen, clutching a bag of salt and vinegar potato chips.

"Do you know anything about this?" I waved a hand at the cool rider on my sofa.

An early Christmas gift from his Uncle Raoul. The

raccoon climbed beside the Yorkie and dug into the bag of chips with gusto.

"Um, I have questions."

Raoul shoved a pawful of chips into his mouth. *I found them at the dump. They were on top of the pile so still clean and in good shape.*

I chose my next words carefully, not wanting to seem ungrateful. "That's very thoughtful, Raoul. Any reason you chose that particular ensemble?"

Raoul cast a sidelong glance at the ancient dog. *Because that's how I see him.*

"As a minor character in *Grease*?"

As too cool for school. PP3 doesn't care what anybody thinks. He does what he wants, when he wants. Now the outside reflects the inside.

I stared at him. "Say that again."

His beady eyes locked on me. *He does what he wants, when he wants. Okay, fine. He needs someone to let him outside to do his business, which is a little lazy...*

"Not that part. The last part."

Now the outside reflects the inside?

"Yes, that." I paced the floor, my mind spilling over with ideas. "Maybe it isn't that Rick and Florian are unaffected by the spell."

But I thought they look the same.

"They do." I spun away from the raccoon and paced the length of the floor. Timothy's faded wings and perpetual hangdog expression. Bertram's fragility. Linnea's small stature. "I think I understand what kind of spell it was."

The kind that freaks out an entire town?

I ignored him. "I think it's showing everyone their visions of themselves and making them a reality. It's produced mirror versions of how we see ourselves."

Then why am I not a lion with a golden mane?

I looked at the raccoon. "Is that how you see yourself?"

Don't sound so surprised.

"I don't think animals like you and PP3 were impacted by the spell. Sorry."

I'm a familiar. These things should affect me.

"You can file a complaint with the caster when we identify them."

My mind continued to race as I considered the changes I was aware of—Aster, Aunt Hyacinth, Linnea, Granger, Bolan, Marley. "That's why some people don't look much different. They're secure with who they are." It made sense that an emotionally healthy minotaur would look exactly the same. Rick was comfortable with himself. Florian too. It also explained the reason Marley looked like a younger version of me—that was how she viewed herself.

Why would anyone do a spell like that on the whole town?

"To cause mischief. As a distraction. Or maybe they didn't mean to. What if they only intended to change themselves and screwed up?"

That's a pretty big screwup.

"If it's a mistake, then we're looking for someone with improvements like Bolan, except capable of magic."

How are we supposed to narrow that down? Break into every therapist's office in town and read their files? He paused. *Because I'm not opposed to that.*

Marley appeared at the base of the stairs. "Hey, Mom. Are you talking about the spell?"

I nodded. "I think I figured out what the changes mean." I explained my theory.

Marley frowned. "I guess that makes sense. I do see myself as a younger version of you."

"If that's true, you should stop doing that. You have a lot more potential than I ever did."

Marley rolled her eyes. "On that note, if the caster messed up the spell, then maybe we're looking for someone who's not particularly good at magic, but they're still powerful enough to affect the whole town."

I aimed a finger at her. "I think you might be onto something. I bet we could come up with a list of paranormals who fall into that category"—I gave Raoul a pointed look—"without the need to commit a crime."

You suck the joy out of life—you know that?

My mind continued trying to make connections. "But what does the spell have to do with Bertram's murder?"

Maybe he felt dead inside, Raoul offered.

I looked at the raccoon. "That's … sad." I shook my head. "But no, he was strangled."

Marley shrugged. "Maybe it's an unfortunate coincidence."

It was possible. Still, the timing seemed too close for comfort. What better way for a murderer to distract from the crime than to spell the whole town? Of course, it would have made more sense to kill him in private. There would've been no need to distract witnesses with a spell if they'd been alone.

"I don't know. Given the timing, I feel like there's a connection between the two events. If we find whoever cast the spell, that might be the quickest way to solve the murder."

You know I'm here to help, even if there's no breaking and entering involved.

"I'm sure you can manage a petty theft at some point during the investigation."

Don't get my hopes up.

I pulled my phone from my pocket and called Deputy Bolan, sharing my thoughts.

"I think you might be onto something, Rose."

"We should check the academy for any students being bullied."

"I can help with that," Marley interjected.

"Why victims of bullying?" Deputy Bolan asked.

"Think about it," I said. "Who would be more eager to change their appearance to the way they view themselves than someone who wants to prove they're better than everybody thinks?"

"I can think of a few students right off the top of my head," Marley said. "The academy is full of bullying."

I scrunched my nose. "Nobody's bothering you, are they?"

She lifted her chin a fraction. "I'm a Rose. Who would dare?"

My family's legacy was good for something at least.

"Marley can handle the academy angle."

"I'll have Deputy Pitt check with the public schools," Bolan said. "I still think Timothy Lapp could be responsible though. I don't think we can safely rule him out."

"He's a fairy," I reminded him. "You said they're not capable of this kind of magic."

"I know, but he could've hired someone who wasn't as adept as they claimed."

"That's true. Who's offering magical services? Anyone with a record or a history of shady spells?"

"I'll look into it," Bolan said.

"I have a source I can tap too. Maybe I should let you talk to her. She has a soft spot for strapping men. What does your husband think of your new look?"

Bolan sighed. "Let's not talk about that."

"He doesn't like this version of you?"

"He doesn't think it suits me. He thinks being small and green is part of my overall appeal."

"You sound disgruntled."

"I feel like he wants to keep me down."

"That doesn't sound like your supportive husband. I think you might be projecting."

"No, this version of me is the projection. This is exactly what I see when I look in the mirror, even before the spell."

"Where'd you get that mirror—the Wish Market?"

He huffed. "We'll talk later." He hung up.

I tucked the phone in my pocket and focused on Marley. "School must be very strange right now."

"It's definitely got a vibe." She flopped on the sofa. "I keep getting mistaken for a teacher. Somebody asked me to cover alchemy because the teacher was out."

I snorted. "I'm surprised anyone would mistake a younger version of me for a teacher." An image flashed in my head of a wingless Bertram Lapp on the floor of the restaurant. "If my theory is right, then Bertram didn't see himself as a fairy. Just an old man in a suit."

"Self-loathing fairy?" Marley queried.

"Could be, or he just wasn't in touch with that side of himself."

"In that case, Granger is way too in touch with his wolf side," Marley said. "He should do something about that."

I gave her a rueful smile. "I'm sure he'd like nothing more."

I pictured tiny Linnea. The small yet adorable monster that was Aspen. Wolf Granger. The more examples I drummed up, the more certain I was that we were dealing with the effects of some kind of mirror spell. The question remained—why?

Chapter Five

I parked in the semicircular driveway of Haverford House. If there was one witch with the key to magical secrets in town, it was Artemis Haverford.

The door opened before I managed to knock. It seemed that her ghostly manservant was already aware of my arrival.

"How are you, Jefferson?"

I felt a gentle breeze dust my arms as I entered the house.

"Hello, Ember, dear. I thought that was your car in the driveway."

I turned at the familiar voice to see an unfamiliar figure. "Artemis?" The elderly witch no longer looked like a skeleton in a moth-eaten wedding dress. Unblemished skin. Long, shiny hair. Youth and beauty had returned to her in full force. "You're an absolute vision."

A blush crept into her cheeks. "You sound like Jefferson. He can't stop raving about me—in his own special way, of course."

"I suppose the spell didn't have any impact on him."

She shook her head. "Sadly not. It's for the best, though. You wouldn't want every ghost in town to be walking around disguised as the living."

I shuddered at the prospect. "Do you know the spell that was cast?"

"From what I've heard, it's some kind of mirror spell, one that reflects the way paranormals view themselves."

"That's my theory, too."

Artemis gave me a cursory glance. "You don't seem much different."

"Are you surprised?"

She laughed lightly. "Actually, yes."

"What would you have expected?"

"I honestly don't know."

"I've developed a few fine lines and wrinkles, if that helps."

"Keep those up, and we'll meet in the middle," she joked. "Would you like a cup of tea?"

"Not today, thanks. I'm here to talk to you about the spell. Deputy Bolan and I are trying to identify magic users capable of conjuring a spell of this magnitude."

Artemis sauntered to the parlor room with an extra swing in her hips and sat on the settee. Clementine, her familiar, luxuriated in a beam of sunlight.

"The curtains are open," I remarked. The interior of Haverford House was usually bathed in darkness. It dawned on me that that was the reason my car had been spotted in the driveway.

"I thought I'd let a little sunshine in for a change. Clementine seems to enjoy it."

The spell seemed to be having more than a physical impact on the elderly witch.

"We think there might be a connection between the

spell and a murder, that the spell might've been done as a distraction," I explained.

Artemis recoiled in horror. "How terrible."

"That's why we're trying to locate the caster. It might help us find the killer."

Artemis shifted uneasily. "And I suppose you'll want to reverse the spell."

"Yes," I said slowly. "Not everyone is stuck in a positive version of themselves." I hesitated. "Granger's a wolf. Linnea is almost too small to function."

"Oh, dear. I can see how Granger's condition might be a problem if there's a murder to be solved."

"Linnea had to cancel the reservations at Palmetto House this week."

Artemis frowned. "How's Marley?"

"Good. Just a younger version of me."

"That's a relief."

"As long as she doesn't start acting like a younger version of me, too."

Artemis laughed. "You're too hard on yourself, Ember. I'm sure you weren't as bad as that."

"My father might tell a different tale, if he were still with us."

"Your father was far too good to raise a wild child."

"That must be where Marley gets her goodness. It skipped a generation, like the gene that lets you roll your tongue."

"Oh, I don't have that one either," she said, "but Jefferson does," she added with a sly wink.

"I need the bathroom," I blurted, desperate to change the subject.

"You remember where it is, don't you?"

I dashed from the parlor and sequestered myself in the

small downstairs powder room. I splashed water on my face to get rid of the obvious signs of embarrassment. As I reached for the hand towel, I glanced at the mirror to check for new wrinkles. A familiar face looked back at me in surprise, except it wasn't mine.

It belonged to Ivy Rose.

"How?" I asked.

Ivy Rose asked the same question at the same time.

I raised my hand. The white-blond witch in the mirror did the same. I shut my eyes and fled the powder room.

"Ember, whatever's the matter?" Artemis asked.

"What do you see when you look at me?"

"A young woman with a very bright future," she declared, giving her knee a firm slap.

"No, I mean physically. I still look like Ember, right?" I touched my head. "Is my hair dark or light?"

Artemis scrutinized me. "Dark. What's this about?"

"I looked at myself in the mirror and saw ... someone else."

"Who, dear?" She sucked in a breath. "Don't tell me you saw Hyacinth. That would give anybody a fright."

"Not my aunt." I inhaled sharply. "Ivy Rose, my ancestor." The ancient witch whose powerful magic I'd acquired when I opened her Book of Shadows.

"How strange. I see you, Ember. As you said, a smidge older, perhaps—but still you."

I sagged with relief as I sat in the chair adjacent to her. It wasn't the spell then, only my subconscious playing tricks on me. It made sense—I didn't think of myself as Ivy. I only worried about the repercussions of holding onto her incredible power.

"Bolan and I are developing a list of magic users strong enough to cast a wide-reaching spell. I thought you might be able to help." Artemis knew much of the gossip that passed from lip to ear in Starry Hollow. Many residents ventured to Haverford House to seek out her wisdom or matchmaking skills and were more than happy to chat about the lives of others during their visit.

"I can think of a number of witches and wizards with the capability but not many with a reason to do so."

"Money? Revenge?"

"Who's the victim?"

"Bertram Lapp."

Her lips puckered. "Oh. I knew Bert. He came to me about six months ago."

That was news. "Why?"

"He was a widow in search of a companion. He didn't like living on his own. He said he missed the companionship of his wife."

"Why didn't he follow up?"

"He said he met someone and was no longer interested in meeting other women."

"Did he mention her name?"

"I'm afraid not. I suppose I should've asked, but it didn't occur to me. I was simply happy that he'd gotten what he wanted. He was nice. He seemed to genuinely miss his wife." Her expression radiated sympathy. "I got the impression that he was lonely, even though he had others in his life."

"He had two sons and a lot of friends," I said. "They attended his seventieth birthday party."

Artemis cringed. "And that's where he died?"

I nodded.

"How dreadful. What kind of sick paranormal chooses to murder someone at his own party?"

"What kind of sick mind chooses to murder someone anywhere at all?"

"Good point."

"I don't suppose he would've mentioned any issues when he was with you," I said.

"No, he was very focused on the task at hand." She smiled. "He was paying me an hourly rate, you see." Her eyes widened. "Olga Rook-Nightshade," she blurted. "There's a name for you."

"I need more than a name."

"Olga's a powerful witch. Got excommunicated from the coven after a spell went awry."

"Must've been pretty serious to get her kicked out."

"It wasn't simply a mistake that rankled the coven, as I recall. It was the intent behind it. Ask your aunt. I'm sure she'll tell you the story better than I can. You know I stick to the periphery."

"True, but you're willing to fill in more blanks than most witches I talk to. My aunt doesn't always see things with the clarity they require."

Artemis beamed at the compliment. Her teeth were whiter and brighter than teeth had any right to be. They were the teeth of someone who'd never taken a sip of tea or a bite of chocolate. The spell definitely had its perks for some residents.

"I honestly don't recall the sordid details, but I know where you can find her if you'd like to go directly to the source."

"She's still local?" I wasn't sure I'd have stayed in Starry Hollow after that. Then again, I'd gotten fired from my job, lost my boyfriend, and excommunicated from Sunday dinners, but I'd refused to leave Rose Cottage. It was possible Olga Rook-Nightshade had a stubborn streak too.

Artemis nodded. "She lives on a farm called Hog Heaven."

"Interesting choice."

"From what I've heard, it suits her."

I couldn't determine whether that was an insult. I guess I'd decide for myself once I entered the gates of Hog Heaven.

Chapter Six

Hog Heaven was located at the southwestern edge of Starry Hollow. I'd never been to a pig farm and had no idea what to expect other than the pigs themselves. I certainly didn't anticipate being greeted by a spotted pig in a pink tutu.

"Is this how you see yourself?" I asked. Raoul would be so jealous to learn a random pig had been impacted by the spell.

"No, Bianca has worn a tutu for years," a voice said.

I glanced up to see a petite woman with fiery red hair and freckled skin. She wore overalls and heavy black boots.

"I'm looking for Olga Rook-Nightshade."

"Congrats. You found her."

"You've swapped your broomstick for a pitchfork, I see."

She snorted. "Something like that. How can I help you?"

"My name is Ember Rose," I began.

Her eyebrows crept up to her hairline. "No relation to Her Majesty, Hyacinth Rose-Muldoon, I take it."

"I'm her niece."

Olga scrutinized my appearance. "How? You look like Snow White in a family of Cinderellas."

It wasn't exactly an insult. "I take after my mother." Although she'd died when I was an infant, I'd seen enough photographs to note the resemblance.

Another pig wandered into view. This one wore tiny yellow rain boots.

Olga followed my gaze. "That's Peppa. She loves traipsing through muddy puddles."

"Do you dress all the pigs?"

"Everybody needs a hobby."

I clearly had no understanding of the purpose of pig farming. I highly doubted you'd lavish a pig with a name and a wardrobe if you planned to turn her into a sausage patty. As much as I wanted to ask, pig farming wasn't the reason for my visit.

"It's unseasonably chilly today," Olga said. "Want to come inside for a hot drink?"

"Sure."

I followed her up the dirt path that led to the rambling farmhouse. White clapboard siding stretched and turned at surprising angles. It seemed like a lot of square footage for one witch.

"Big house," I commented.

Olga wiped the soles of her boots on the plain welcome mat and opened the door. "It belonged to a farming family before me. There were seven of them. Kids worked the land alongside their parents."

I entered the house behind her. "What happened to them?"

"The parents got too old to keep up the physical labor, and the kids didn't have any interest in farming. I bought it for a good price after…" She stopped midsentence. "You're a Rose. I guess you know what happened to me."

"Generally speaking." I hesitated to ask my next question. "Why pigs?"

She pursed her lips. "Why not? They're smarter than most folks I know. Sweeter too."

I sensed it was more than that. "Does your familiar mind?" I craned my neck in search of a cat.

"My familiar is no longer with me, but she wouldn't have minded." Olga filled the kettle with water and padded to the stovetop. "Her name was Frankie, and she was a pig."

Now I understood. "Frankie as in frankfurter?"

Olga nodded. "She was the plumpest thing you've ever seen. Her stomach looked like she was about to give birth to three bowling balls." The witch smiled at the memory of her beloved familiar. "She waddled after me everywhere I went, but it made no difference how much she walked. She kept putting on the pounds."

"That's an unusual familiar."

Olga's face tightened. "You're not going to judge me, are you? Because the door's right there." She inclined her head toward the kitchen door.

"Not at all. My familiar's a raccoon."

Olga's brow lifted. "Are you mocking me?"

"Nope. His name is Raoul. He loves pizza, dumpster diving, and bossing me around."

Olga pressed her palm flat against her chest as a tiny gasp escaped her. "Frankie loved trash. And mud. I used to call her my little trashy dirtbag." She paused. "I meant it as a term of endearment, of course."

I was almost afraid to ask my next question. "What happened to her?"

Olga's eyes misted over. "I'd rather not talk about it.

Suffice it to say, when the opportunity arose, I decided to create Hog Heaven in her honor."

A pig ambled into the kitchen and grunted at us before settling down on the braided rug by the sink. He wore a tiny horned helmet.

Olga's gaze flicked to the interloper. "That's Wilbur. He's a Vikings fan."

"The historic culture or the football team?"

"Can it be both?" She filled two mugs with hot water and dropped in two teabags.

"So it's only you here and a herd of pigs?"

"Just the way I like it," she said. "Milk and sugar?"

"One teaspoon of sugar. No milk."

Olga delivered the mugs to the table and pushed the sugar bowl toward me.

"Were you affected by the spell?" I didn't know enough about her to notice any differences.

She dunked her teabag. "What spell?"

"The spell that affected the whole town. You haven't heard anything about it?"

"No, but that explains why you're here. I suppose the coven thinks I'm responsible."

"Why would you assume that?"

She cut a quick glance at me. "You know why."

"I only know that you were excommunicated. I don't have a long history here. Why don't you enlighten me?"

Olga took a long sip from her mug before answering. "Where are you from?"

"I was born here but raised in New Jersey."

She broke into a smile. "I love the Garden State. Some of the best music has come out of that place."

Something we agreed on. "Are you a Springsteen fan?"

She seemed incredulous. "Is anybody *not* a Springsteen fan?"

"Lots of people, actually, but I don't want to know them." My father had been an ardent Springsteen fan and had passed his love down to me.

"If you want to know whether I cast the spell, the answer is no. I don't practice magic anymore." Olga delivered the tea to the table.

"Why not?"

"Because I didn't like the way it made me feel."

Interesting response. "How did it make you feel?"

She blew out a breath. "After I was kicked out of the coven, I took a hard look at my behavior and realized that I'd let magic take control my life. It was almost like an addiction."

"And you decided to wean yourself off?"

"I stopped cold turkey, which probably wasn't the smartest thing to do. I had no support system in place." She glanced at the pig sprawled across the rug. "My pigs saved me."

"How so?"

"This place takes effort to maintain. The pigs are a lot of work. I basically started monotasking. I'd focus on one job at a time and give it my full attention."

I thought of my ancestor, Ivy Rose, and the difficulties she'd faced with her powerful magic. Maybe if she'd had a pig farm or access to the internet to learn about monotasking, her life would've turned out differently.

"Do you know the name Bertram Lapp?"

She shook her head. "Should I?"

"He was murdered when the spell was cast. We're trying to determine if there's a connection or if it's unfortunate timing."

She cocked her head. "Are you a cop?"

"A private investigator, but the sheriff hires me as a consultant." I fiddled with the handle of my mug. "Would you mind telling me what happened with the coven?"

Her eyes narrowed. "You still think I might've been involved in the spell?"

"Not necessarily."

Olga observed me for a moment, then blew out a sigh of acquiescence. "I didn't mean to hurt anybody. The spell was supposed to be limited to one witch."

"How many did it affect?"

She shrugged. "About a dozen."

I now understood why Artemis had suggested her.

"There was a May Day dance in the woods. The wizard I was interested in was going, but so was the slutty witch who'd set her sights on him as her next conquest."

"Let me guess. You decided to use magic to get her out of the way."

"I brought a potion with me. I stood behind her and spritzed it in the air. It was only meant to affect her."

"What happened?"

"It affected everybody in the clearing, including me. We couldn't stop dancing. At first it was funny." Her expression darkened. "It didn't take long to become serious. The wizard I liked broke his leg. The slutty witch danced her way into a swamp and nearly drowned. It took half the coven to break the spell. I couldn't help because I was affected. My trainee was the one who ran for help. I felt guilty for involving her in the first place."

"You had a trainee?"

"Sort of. She struggled with certain aspects of her magic. I was the witch assigned to tutor her. Some role model I was."

I felt an immediate kinship with her. "I had a whole stable of tutors."

"Really? Why would a Rose need tutors? You're the descendant of the One True Witch."

"Because I knew nothing about magic when I came here. My father hid this world from me. I didn't even know he was a wizard until after he died."

Olga's expression softened. "I'm sorry to hear that. Must've been quite a shock."

"I've had a lot of shocks in my life. You get used to them."

A small smile crossed her lips. "Who'd they have tutoring you? Wren?"

"Yes."

"Marigold, I bet. And Hazel."

"That's right. And Ian." I sipped my tea. "What was your specialty?"

"Any advanced spell, really. I was the kind of witch that bumbled my way through the basics but came into my own as spells grew more complex."

"That's unusual."

"It is. Magical dyspraxia, they called it."

"Who?"

"The coven. Ever hear of dyspraxia?"

I shook my head.

"It affects the right side of the brain. If the same disruptions happened on the left side, you'd be dyslexic. Depending on the person, you might have trouble with fine motor skills or basic mathematical computations like multiplication but excel at calculus."

The brain never ceased to amaze me.

"So you have the magical equivalent?"

She shrugged. "Seemed to be the case. When I was

younger, the coven was sure I was going to be a failure. They couldn't understand why I failed to master basic tasks. My parents would get so frustrated with me. Punishment never worked. It was only as I grew older, and the material got harder that I began to shine. That's one reason I offered to help Enid, because I thought she was like me."

I couldn't imagine how difficult that must've been for Olga, to try her best and not understand the reasons behind her inability.

"That wasn't my situation. I was bad at the basics because I didn't have any experience at all."

She looked at me. "And now?"

I didn't want to get into the story of Ivy Rose. "I'm focused on earning a living and raising my daughter."

"You have a daughter?"

"Her name is Marley. She started at the public school before she came into her magic, but now she attends the Black Cloak Academy."

"No doubt. Which wizard did you marry? I bet you had your choice of suitors. Everybody wants a piece of the Roses."

"Karl was human. We grew up in New Jersey together."

Olga whistled. "That must be a sore subject for Hyacinth."

"It was, but my aunt has changed a lot since you knew her."

"That seems unlikely. Your aunt was as cold and hard as ice. Can't see anything melting her."

"You should come to a coven meeting. See for yourself."

She grunted. "I was expelled, remember? I'm not welcome to walk among them. Anyway, I don't practice magic, and it's probably best not to be around it so I'm not tempted to start again."

That I understood. "I'm sorry about what happened to you." I knew what it was like to feel like an outsider, an outcast. It was unpleasant at the best of times.

"I appreciate you saying that." She pushed her chair back, scraping the legs against the pine floorboards. "Come on. Wilbur and I will walk you out."

She opened the door and light flooded the kitchen. She angled her head, staring at mine. "Have you always had that shock of white hair? I didn't notice it when you came in."

My throat felt lumpy. I thought my changes had been limited to fine lines and wrinkles. "It's the spell," I forced out. "If you think of anything that might help us, will you let me know?" I handed her my business card.

She studied the card. "R&R?"

"My familiar is Raoul. He's my partner. I thought it would be best to leave him at home. I wasn't sure how the pigs would respond to him."

She laughed. "Did you worry I might be wearing one of his relatives as a hat? It's not the frontier."

I gazed at her for a moment, standing on her porch with her overalls and a Viking pig at her side. "You seem happy, Olga. Content."

Olga's smile widened. "I am. It isn't the life I pictured for myself, but once I committed to it, I felt a sense of peace. I like working with my hands. Simple tasks. I can fix my own toilet. Unclog my sink. All sorts of jobs—and without the use of magic." Her chest puffed with pride. "Hog Heaven has become my idea of nirvana."

I felt a pang of envy. Maybe one day I'd reach that level of contentment. But today was not that day.

Today I had a murder to solve.

Chapter Seven

As promised, Marley and Deputy Pitt had gathered a short list of names from the schools, but the suspects had all been in the presence of others when the spell hit and seemed genuinely baffled by recent events.

Bolan and I decided to split up again. This time he went to interview another guest from the party, one of Bertram's neighbors. He assigned me to another attendee, the victim's best friend, Eugene Dalton. I brought Raoul as backup.

I found Eugene in a workshop behind his house. He sat at a table with his back to me. The small outbuilding was filled with clocks.

This guy either has a serious hobby or a weird fetish, Raoul said.

The clocks ranged from cuckoo to grandfather. Their faces were designed with a variety of backgrounds, including planets, flowers, and an owl. I became so mesmerized that I almost forgot the reason for my visit until Raoul nudged my leg.

"Eugene Dalton?"

He spun his chair toward me. He was average build with a head of luxurious brown hair. "That's me." He peered at me over the rim of his glasses. "Do I know you?"

"No, sir. My name is Ember Rose." I entered the workshop and handed him my business card. "I'm investigating the death of Bertram Lapp. I'm sorry. I know you and he were close friends."

He didn't respond. Instead, he shifted his attention to Raoul. "Is this your deputy?"

"I'm not the sheriff, Mr. Dalton."

"Then why are you doing the sheriff's job?" He passed the card back to me. "I'm not speaking to some random PI that brings her pet to work."

Raoul stiffened. *Who's he calling a pet?*

"As you can imagine, Mr. Dalton, the sheriff's office is very busy thanks to the mirror spell. The phone won't stop ringing."

He chuckled. "Is that what they're calling it? I guess that makes sense." He gave me an appraising look. "What are your changes?"

"Only minor, surprisingly."

He retrieved his phone and scrolled until he landed on a photo. He turned the screen so I could see it. It was Eugene Dalton with a bald head.

"You see yourself with hair," I said.

He nodded. "I lost my hair in my twenties, but I still look in the mirror and see the guy I used to be. Sometimes I'd even forget I was bald until someone commented on it. My wife met me when I was clinging to the last of my hair. She didn't mind it, though. Told me hair doesn't make the man." He raked a hand through his thick head of hair. "I believed her, until now. This spell has shown me what a difference it truly makes."

"In what way?"

He blew a dismissive breath. "How much time do you have? Ladies that wouldn't give me a sideways look are now staring me down."

"What about your wife?"

"She died two years ago. She'd been sick for two years before that. Took me some time to adjust, but I decided the single life doesn't suit me. I like having someone."

I could relate to that. Although I was accustomed to being single and independent, I preferred having a partner, preferably one that didn't leave fur on the sheets. I looked forward to the breaking of the spell.

"I'm a widow," I told him. "My husband died in an accident years ago."

"I'm sorry to hear that." He looked me up and down. "You must've gotten married pretty young."

"I did. Got pregnant pretty young, too."

He chuckled. "You ever meet someone else?"

"Eventually." Not without a few bumps in the road, though.

"It's nice, isn't it? You think you'll never love again, and then ... bam! Hits you when you least expect it."

I hadn't expected it, but I also hadn't been ready for it when it initially happened with Granger. As much as I hated the pain and suffering that accompanied my relationship with Alec, though, I wasn't sure I would've arrived at my present state without that experience.

"What's her name?" I asked.

"Carly Santana. Bert and I met her at a birthday party the same night. I guess you know Bert was a widower, too."

I nodded. "Did you know his wife?"

"Of course. Bert and I were best friends for thirty years. Our wives were friends, too. Marilyn was a real sweet woman. Would make you a casserole if you had a bad day and knit you a sweater if she thought you looked chilly."

"She sounds lovely."

Eugene's head tilted, and he stared into space. "She was. We all took it hard when she died. It was one of the reasons I debated whether to make a move on Carly. Bert needed someone more than I did, and he hadn't shown interest in anybody until she came along."

That was unfortunate. "She must be a special lady."

He inhaled deeply. "Carly is a gift from the gods."

"Was she dating both of you?"

"Not technically. The three of us spent a lot of time together as a trio. Wasn't the healthiest dynamic, but neither of us was willing to cede to the other."

"What about Carly? What did she think of the situation?"

He scratched his head. "Don't know. I never asked her."

My mouth fell open. "You and Bertram were competing for a woman, and you never bothered to ask her opinion as to which one of you she preferred?"

"I guess we didn't want to know the answer."

"And now?" I prompted.

"Now I don't have to ask. Process of elimination." He didn't smile. "I'm not happy he's dead, of course. He was my best friend. But I'm glad he didn't have to feel the sting of rejection."

Only because Bertram Lapp didn't have to feel anything at all. I wasn't sure that was better.

"Can I ask where you were when Bertram was killed? I know you attended the party."

He fixed me with a hard stare. "Are you asking me if I had anything to do with the murder of my best friend?"

Lifting my chin, I met his gaze. "Yes."

"I would never have hurt him, not for a woman or any other reason. Anyway, I couldn't have killed him because I was unconscious. I ran into the dining room to see what the screams were about and saw the giant rat. I ran straight out the nearest exit to get away and tripped. Knocked myself unconscious. When I came to, I went directly to the healer's office to make sure I didn't have a concussion. I didn't find out Bert died until later."

"Which healer's office?"

He gave me the name and number. "It was crowded, but they'll remember I was there. I threw up in the waiting room."

"You had a concussion then?"

Nodding, he raked a hand through his lush hair. "It's going to be one of those moments that everybody will remember exactly where they were and what they were doing when the spell hit."

"Any idea who might have wanted Bertram dead?"

Eugene scratched behind his ear. "All his nearest and dearest were at the party. I can't imagine anybody there wanting to hurt him. Are you sure it wasn't an accident?"

"He was strangled, Mr. Dalton. I don't see how putting your hands around someone's neck and squeezing until they die could be an accident."

He fell silent.

"Can you walk me through Bertram's week leading up to the party? Anything stand out to you?"

Eugene made a popping sound with his lips as he considered the question. "He had an appointment with his lawyer last week, but it was nothing unusual. A minor update to his will that he'd been putting off ever since Marilyn died."

I perked up. "A will update?"

"Nothing noteworthy. Just modifying some language that was affected by his wife's death. He was still dividing his estate between the boys, same as before."

"And his sons knew this?"

"Bert's always been open with them about his plans. He figured if they knew up front they were each getting half, there'd be no resentment. He was very keen on the boys getting along. I think it bothered him that they never really bonded."

"Not all siblings do," I said, thinking of Granger and Wyatt.

"Jeremiah takes after Bert, and Timothy takes after Marilyn. Funny how the pairing worked well for a married couple but not so much for brothers."

"They're not carbon copies. They're going to be influenced by their own relationships and experiences."

"True."

At that moment, a dozen cuckoos burst out of their clocks. Raoul ran from the outbuilding like his tail was on fire.

"I don't know who he takes after," I joked.

"You should talk to Tyler Adams. The young elf that worked for him."

"Any particular reason?"

Eugene shrugged. "Bert treated him like a son. Maybe Tyler resented that the treatment wouldn't extend to his will. Worth a conversation anyway."

It definitely was.

"I can't handle you looking like me much longer," I said, gazing at Marley across the room. I'd spent all of dinner trying not to look at her. Now she was planted at the table

Magic & Mirrors

in the living room, scrutinizing her homework with my younger face.

"Sounds like self-loathing to me," she said. She returned her attention to the book in front of her.

"It's not self-loathing. It's weird."

A knock on the door interrupted us. I was shocked to see Aunt Hyacinth on my doorstep. She swept past me and entered the cottage.

"We're going to try to override the spell," she announced. "I assume you'd like to partake."

"Yes, of course." I paused. "Who's we?"

"The Silver Moon coven. Who else?"

"You have a counterspell?"

"We hope so. We've had a team assigned to crafting one all day."

Of course they did. "It's a good idea. Is there any way to trace the spell to its originator?"

"That's a secondary concern. The priority right now is undoing the damage."

"Not when you have a killer to catch."

My aunt leveled me with a look. "If you're too preoccupied with this hobby of yours, then we'll simply perform the spell without you." She paused, drawing breath. "Forgive me. I meant to say your job. Obviously, it's not a hobby."

"No, it pays my bills now." Ever since I was fired from my job as a reporter at *Vox Populi*, the weekly newspaper owned by Aunt Hyacinth. There was no need to say the words out loud. My aunt was aware of her role in my abrupt career change.

"Grab your cloak, and let's go. We're meeting at the ritual spot in the woods in fifteen minutes."

I studied her for a moment. "This is very altruistic of you."

"A spell has overtaken the entire town. Who do you think will be blamed for such an event?"

"I see." Spin control. I should've known. Still, she wasn't wrong. Tensions could rise between members of the coven and everybody else if it was believed the coven was responsible.

"Can I go?" Marley piped up.

"Of course," my aunt replied.

"Really? Isn't she too young?"

"She's a Rose," my aunt said, as though that explained it.

Marley and I donned our cloaks and accompanied Aunt Hyacinth to the clearing.

The moon shone against the darkening sky like a coin in a puddle. My shoes crunched through the leaves on the forest floor.

No sneaking up on your enemies in this part of the woods, Raoul lamented.

I'll make sure to include that in my battle plans, I replied. A chill settled over us, and I stuffed my hands into the deep pockets of my cloak.

"This is so exciting," Marley said. She wore her Silver Moon cloak, affixed with a silver rose broach. "My friends at school will be so jealous."

"I wouldn't flaunt it," I warned her.

"They'd understand it was because of Aunt Hyacinth and nothing to do with them not being good enough. My friends are pretty secure."

"Teach me their ways," I joked.

By the time we reached the clearing, dozens of dark cloaks swarmed the area. I noticed a handful of witches and wizards who'd been impacted by the spell. Even the High Priestess, Iris Sandstone, had a head of frizzy hair.

Gardenia, the scribe, was scrolling on her phone. At first I thought she was reviewing notes for the ritual until I caught a glimpse of a cat video on the screen.

Magnus Destry, the High Priest, approached us to greet Aunt Hyacinth. "This spell has provided us with quite the opportunity to come together as a coven."

"Have you been writing in your gratitude journal again?" I asked.

Magnus didn't crack a smile.

"What's with you? You're usually chattier than this."

He opened his mouth, revealing a set of horribly crooked teeth. "I shall never be critical of my appearance again."

"That's your secret shame? British teeth?"

"I never realized how poorly I thought of my teeth until now. I must give credit to the caster. The spell made me very conscious of my inner critic."

"My inner critic lives next door," I replied, jabbing a thumb in my aunt's direction.

"You seem more or less as you are," Magnus said.

"You sound surprised."

The blast of a horn drew our attention to the circle.

Iris glanced at Gardenia. "Did you apply for the emergency permit?"

"I thought Zahara was doing it."

Zahara looked at them with a blank expression. "I thought Calla was doing it."

"Calla can't remember where she left her dentures."

My aunt threw up her hands in frustration. "Let's get on with it and hope we don't run into another group."

I knew which group she meant—the werewolf pack had a tendency to disrupt coven activities even when we'd filed the right paperwork.

Argyle Pennywhistle hobbled over to see us. I generally avoided the coven purse warden because he only wanted to speak to me when my dues were late.

"Ember, so glad to see you out and about," the elderly wizard said. "I missed you at the last coven meeting."

"Really?" I said, knowing perfectly well I'd dodged him by the cookie table. "I don't know how." There'd been a cookie with my name on it that ended up in Florian's greedy hand, not that I was holding a grudge.

Argyle rubbed his balding head. "Your dues are late again."

I feigned ignorance. "Are you sure?"

"Quite."

"What's this?" Aunt Hyacinth poked her head between us. "Did I hear you say Yarrow's dues are late?"

Argyle cleared his throat, clearly not excited to tell Hyacinth Rose-Muldoon that her niece had disgraced the family once again. "I'm sure it's merely an oversight. I thought I'd mention it since we're here together."

"I'll have the money to you soon," I said. Truth be told, I was behind on a few payments because of my change in circumstances. Nothing dire, but I didn't want anybody to know, especially Marley. I was no stranger to struggling to make ends meet, although I'd been hopeful that our move to Starry Hollow would put an end to all that. At least we had a roof over our heads that couldn't be taken away. Rose Cottage had belonged to my parents, and I'd inherited the house free and clear.

As soon as Argyle shuffled away to harass another delinquent witch, my aunt tugged my cloak sleeve. "Why didn't you tell me you're having financial difficulties?"

The stubborn and prideful part of me took center stage. "Because I'm not. I just like to give Argyle a hard time."

Her eyes narrowed. "If you require assistance, I'd be more than willing to bridge the gap until you're in a better position."

"Is that guilt talking, or are you afraid I'll drag the family's good name through the mud?" I asked.

"Does it matter?"

"I guess not," I mumbled.

"Your business is still new. It will take time to build."

"It didn't take Aster time. Sidhe Shed was an instant success."

"And you had the opportunity to join her in that endeavor, but you chose to travel your own path," she said, "which I fully support. That wasn't meant as an admonishment. I admire that you don't rely on others to sustain you." Her gaze flicked to Florian. "If only other family members were as determined to be self-sufficient."

Florian leaned over to me and whispered, "Have you seen Delphine? Great gods above, I dodged a bullet with that one."

I scanned the crowd for any sign of the pretty librarian. "I don't think she's here."

"Oh, she's here. Look to your three o'clock."

I panned across the sea of cloaks and settled on a tall, gangly witch with greasy hair and a wart at the end of her long nose. The only feature I recognized were her eyes. "What did the spell do to her?" I whispered, more to myself.

"If the spell reveals our true natures, Wren might want to reconsider their relationship."

I smacked my cousin's arm. "It doesn't reveal our true natures. It reveals the way we view ourselves."

"Close enough," Florian replied.

The spell involved a lot of chanting, a stinky mixture of herbs, and enough candles to burn down the entire forest.

Unfortunately, it didn't work. The team involved in crafting the spell apologized profusely.

"It's all right," my aunt said, in a rare display of magnanimity. "I felt resistance. I think it needs to be broken by the caster."

I'd felt resistance too, although I hadn't recognized it as such until my aunt mentioned it. If I'd realized, I might've pushed harder. Then again, it wouldn't have mattered if Aunt Hyacinth was right about the spell needing to be broken by the caster.

The failed spell only strengthened my resolve to find the one responsible, if for no other reason than to restore Delphine's good looks. Florian was right—that wart alone needed its own zip code.

"Good team effort," Aunt Hyacinth called over her shoulder as we vacated the forest.

Marley and I exchanged looks. It seemed the outside of my aunt wasn't the only part affected by the spell. Maybe I'd ask the caster to tweak the reversal spell to allow paranormals to retain some of the better qualities.

But first I had to find them.

Chapter Eight

The Caffeinated Cauldron was bustling the next morning. It was so crowded, in fact, that I had to wait for someone to leave before I could enter the building because the line went all the way to the door.

The patron in front of me turned around and grimaced. If I'd been paying closer attention, I would've noticed the bright red curls. Once she pivoted to face me, her signature smeared red lipstick was a dead giveaway.

"Good morning, Hazel," I said. "Missed you last night."

"Maybe if I'd been there, we could've reversed the spell."

I realized with a start that Hazel looked the same and felt a mixture of shock and respect. The crazed clown was content with herself. Go figure.

"What kept you? Hot date?"

"That's none of your business."

Her absence might explain her unadulterated look. "Too bad you missed all the fun. This mirror spell is quite revealing. Have you seen Bolan yet? Trust me, you won't recognize him."

"Oh, I was here when the spell was cast. I went to see a friend that lives off the grid afterward. I thought he might be able to help with the reversal, but no such luck."

"You couldn't call or video chat?"

"He's the paranoid type. A discussion could only be had in person and only if you know how to find him."

Now I was curious about her mysterious friend "Who is he?" The line continued to progress toward the counter.

"A wizard named Pollock. We attended Angel Oak University together. He lived a block from me until about ten years ago."

"Why did he leave town?"

Hazel stared at me from beneath a furrowed brow. "Someone's taken her nosy pill this morning."

"Pardon me, Madam of Mystery."

"If you must know, he didn't exactly leave town. He lives in an underground bunker at the border."

"He's waiting for the apocalypse or a zombie invasion? Maybe both?"

"He prefers a life of solitude. Pollock tried the 'normal life' thing for a bit. He'd even wanted the position of High Priest and was unhappy when he was passed over."

"Let me guess—he thought it was a conspiracy and that he should've gotten the position." The wrong order at the drive-thru was a conspiracy against you when you were paranoid.

"He believed there was a faction of the coven working against him, yes. He withdrew from society."

"Sounds like an overreaction."

Hazel snorted. "You should see the bunker."

"Why was he passed over if he's so talented?" I didn't disbelieve her. The fact that Hazel went out of her way to seek his assistance meant he was the real deal. She didn't suffer fools gladly.

"He wasn't entirely wrong about the factions. You know how these things can be. Sometimes appointments and elections are nothing more than a high school popularity contest. Pollock is incredibly skilled, but he lacks finesse. Makes it hard to warm to him."

"No wonder you two get along so well."

Finally, it was Hazel's turn at the counter. She placed her order and gestured to me. "And whatever she's having as well."

"Someone's feeling generous today. Thanks, Hazel." I joined her at the counter and ordered a medium latte with a shot of progress.

"How's the sheriff?" she asked in a quiet voice. "I heard he's one of the more affected cases."

"He's frustrated, I think. There's a murder to solve, and he has to pant helplessly from the sidelines."

The barista passed our cups across the counter, and we headed toward the exit.

"A fairy, wasn't it?"

I nodded. "Bertram Lapp. Still not sure whether that part's a coincidence. Did Pollock have any thoughts on the spell?"

Hazel stopped to cover her cup with a lid. "Well, he doesn't think it's fairy magic, if that helps you."

Neither did I. "He thinks it's one of us?"

"He thinks it's a witch, specifically."

"But not a wizard? Why not?"

Hazel shrugged. "He doesn't explain. He only spews. It's all very stream of consciousness. He said a spell like this is akin to using poison."

"A woman's weapon?"

"More or less. He thinks a wizard wouldn't gravitate to a spell involving appearances."

"Unless the spell was accidental, which we still haven't ruled out. I'm surprised Pollock didn't give you a counter-spell to try."

"He was concerned that a failed attempt might do more harm than good. I worried when Marigold told me about the coven's effort, that it might end poorly, but it seems like nothing came of it."

"I wouldn't say that. I think Ian got poison ivy."

Hazel smirked. "An unexpected bonus."

We exited the coffee shop. "I'm meeting Bolan to interview a murder suspect."

"I don't suppose you'd like to put a runework lesson on the calendar."

I tapped my ear. "What's that, Hazel?" I made static noises. "I think we have a bad connection. Gotta go." I turned and hustled along the sidewalk toward the shed that served as the home office of R&R Investigations, courtesy of Aster's Sidhe Shed company. Its location adjacent to Granger's office was convenient for both personal and professional reasons. I made sure to finish my latte before I went next door. If you went in there holding one coffee cup and none for anybody else, you were basically asking for a parking ticket.

Deputy Valentina Pitt was behind the desk when I breezed through the door of the sheriff's office, empty-handed. The deputy and I were on good terms, despite her crush on Granger.

"Hey," she greeted me in a flat voice. No surprise she looked exactly the same.

"Is Bolan here yet? I'm supposed to meet him."

"He's in the conference room looking through files. I

heard you're going to interview the mentee today."

"You mean the protégé?"

She shrugged. "What's the difference?"

"One is French and sounds more sophisticated."

The deputy's mouth curved in a subtle smile. "Tyler Adams, right? I glanced at his file. It's pretty thin, like he appeared fully formed."

"He's Starry Hollow's own Athena," I joked.

Deputy Pitt stared at me blankly.

"The goddess was born in full warrior mode straight from Zeus's head," I explained. "Never mind."

Bolan strode into the lobby. There was a confidence to his walk that wasn't present in his smaller, greener form. "You ready to go, Rose?"

"If you're too busy, I'd be happy to go instead," Pitt volunteered.

Bolan gave her a sharp look. "You're not getting out of parking meter enforcement."

Her face fell.

Bolan shifted his attention to me. "I'll drive."

"Are you sure? My car is right outside." I'd noticed the coveted spot and decided to snag it, then walked to the coffee shop.

"I don't care if your car is parked in the lobby, I've seen the way you drive. I've pulled you over, in fact."

Pitt stifled a laugh.

"There's nothing wrong with my driving," I insisted.

Bolan cast a sidelong glance at me. "Maybe in New Jersey. We have higher standards in Starry Hollow."

"You also have less traffic." I hurried to fall in step with Bolan as he exited the building. "Have you been practicing your swagger? Because I hate to admit it, but you're getting really good at it."

Bolan kept his gaze straight ahead. "Maybe a little," he admitted. "You sure it doesn't look like I'm trying too hard?"

"Not at all. Very natural."

He seemed to grow another inch on the way to his car. I climbed into the passenger seat and buckled my seatbelt before he could remind me. Driving with Bolan was like driving with my father.

"Are we going to Tyler's office?" I asked.

Bolan started the car. "Nope. He agreed to meet us at a place nearby. He didn't want his co-workers to see him being questioned."

"Then why not come to the sheriff's office?"

"Because he didn't want anybody to see him there and assume the worst."

Tyler seemed as paranoid as Pollock. "Where are we meeting him then?"

"You'll see."

We drove along the coastline and eventually turned right. "Are those llamas?" I asked.

"Alpacas." Bolan parked in the small lot adjacent to the pasture. "It's a brewery called Three Alpacas."

"Interesting choice for a meeting."

"The place is open but not likely to have customers yet. Pretty smart if you ask me."

We entered the brewery. Sure enough, there was only one guy seated on a bench at a table. Average build. Average height. The kind of bland, average features that would allow him to blend in anywhere and be quickly forgotten.

"You must be Tyler Adams," I said.

"Yeah. Are you the deputy?" The young man cupped his hands around a glass filled with amber liquid. It seemed that someone needed his liquid courage. Wonder why.

"My name is Ember Rose. I'm a consultant."

"And I'm Deputy Bolan." The non-leprechaun sat on the opposite bench across the table.

Beads of sweat formed on Tyler's forehead. "I guess this is about what happened to Bert."

I sat beside Bolan. "It is."

Tyler dragged his sleeve across his damp brow. "Okay, ask your questions."

Bolan studied him. "You seem nervous, Mr. Adams. What do you have to be so nervous about?"

Tyler swallowed hard. "Murder is the kind of thing that makes a person nervous. Maybe not you two because you're used to it."

"Innocent folks don't tend to get nervous," Bolan replied.

I whispered, "That's not strictly true. It depends on the circumstances."

Bolan ignored me. "Let's talk about the dinner party."

"It was a nice evening ... until it wasn't." He stared into his beer. "I've tried to block it from my memory. The whole thing's been pretty traumatic."

"Did you see Mr. Lapp collapse?" I asked.

"No, I ran to the bathroom as soon as the spell hit."

"Why did you do that?" I asked.

Tyler swilled his beer. "I felt sick."

"Did you follow Timothy there?" Bolan asked.

Tyler blinked. "Timothy? No. I didn't notice him. It was pandemonium in the restaurant though. Everybody was freaking out. There was a giant rat."

I turned to Bolan. "Have we heard anything more about the rat?"

"Under sedation until the spell is broken."

Poor guy.

"I went straight into a stall in the bathroom, and then I

went home," Tyler continued. "I didn't find out Bert was dead until later."

I scrutinized his nervous demeanor. His beer was nearly empty; the sweating had stopped, but now his hands were trembling. "Why did you go home without checking on the other dinner guests first?"

"I wasn't thinking clearly. Like I said, it was nuts inside, and I didn't feel well. I'm pretty sure I tripped Carly on my way to the bathroom." He grimaced. "I didn't even look back to see if she was okay."

"She was okay," Bolan said, "other than the same fear and panic everyone else was experiencing." The deputy decided to change tacks. "Any recent problems with your boss at work?"

"None. Bert was a great mentor. I appreciated everything he did for me. If anything, it's bad for me that he's dead. Now I might have to switch departments."

"You won't get promoted to his job?" I asked.

Tyler barked a laugh. "Are you kidding? I'll need years more experience before I'm ready for his position. Bert was a legend at the office. They'll probably move me to accounting until they find someone to fill Bert's role." Tyler groaned. "I hate math."

"I understand Bertram treated you like a son," I said. "Did he happen to confide in you about his plans for his will?"

"His will?" Tyler recoiled. "We didn't have in-depth conversations like that. Too personal. We tended to stick to sports and work."

So much for a motive. "Did Bertram ever mention why he continued to work at his age?" I asked. Based on his financial records that Bolan acquired, he could've retired years ago.

"The subject came up every now and then. He liked to keep busy. His sons are grown, and then his wife died. I got the impression that work felt more like home than his actual house did."

"It's probably hard to leave a place where you're referred to as a legend," Bolan added.

Tyler's head bobbed. "Couldn't blame him. Every morning he'd walk down the corridor past all the assistants' desks and fist bump each one along the way. He was the office celebrity." Tyler bowed his head. "Man, I'm really going to miss him. The office won't be the same without him."

"I have another question," I began. "Our records indicate you're an elf, but your ears aren't pointy."

His fingers absently grazed his lobe. "The effect of the mirror spell. I used to get mocked for my pointy ears at school. I guess I always wished they were more like everybody else's."

"Where did you go to school?" Bolan asked. "I didn't see that information in your file."

His foot started tapping the floor. Another nervous gesture. "It was a mixed school," he said. "We had all kinds of paranormals. Minotaurs, centaurs, fairies..."

I gestured to his head. "In that case, those ears wouldn't have looked like everybody else's."

Bolan looked at me. "What's your point, Rose? Look at me. I went to a mixed school, but this is still what I see in the mirror."

I knew I should drop the subject, but something was spurring me to press on. "Is there anything else different about you except your ears?"

Tyler shifted uncomfortably. "I guess not. So what? You heard what the deputy said."

No. His ears were more significant than that. I felt it in my gut. He might not be nervous about the murder, but he was nervous about *something*. "What's the name of the school you attended?"

"I moved here when I was nineteen," he said.

"That doesn't answer my question." Now I felt certain Tyler was hiding something about his past.

Bolan seemed to agree because he leaned forward and said, "Where'd you go to school, Tyler?"

Tyler swallowed the last of his beer. "You've never heard of it. It's nowhere near here."

"I'd like to look it up," Bolan said.

Tyler's gaze darted toward the exit. He seemed to be debating whether to make a break for it.

"I might not run very fast," I said, "but my magic would put your butt right back on this bench."

He clutched his stomach. "I feel sick."

Bolan assessed him. "Seems to be an issue for you. Might want to get that checked out at the healer's office."

Tyler's face paled. "Fine, I'll confess" he blurted.

Bolan and I exchanged looks.

"Confess to what?" I asked.

"I graduated from Asheville High School. Happy now?" He buried his face in his hands.

"Asheville?" Bolan tugged his earlobe. "Is that near Rainbow Falls?"

I stared at Tyler. "Asheville, North Carolina?"

Tyler didn't look up. "Yeah."

"Why'd your family live in the human world?" Bolan asked.

I watched Tyler carefully. "Because," I said slowly, "they're human. Tyler isn't an elf."

Bolan laughed. "Don't be ridiculous, Rose. It says so in

his file."

I didn't take my eyes off Tyler. His guilty expression told me what I needed to know. "You have the Sight, don't you?"

Tyler nodded. "Took me years to understand what it was. Apparently, my grandmother had it too, but she took off when I was little, so nobody was ever willing to talk about her."

Bolan started to sputter. "You mean Rose is right? You're actually human?"

Tyler tapped the outside of the glass. "I discovered Starry Hollow by accident when I was in college. My buddies didn't have the Sight. They thought I was on hallucinogens when I told them about this magical town I'd seen. As far as they could tell, it was all empty space."

"You got across the bridge?" I asked. My three cousins had whisked me away to the magical town via their own magic, but I'd used the regular entrance since then.

"I snuck across the border," Tyler admitted. "I knew right there and then that I wanted to spend the rest of my life here. It's like living in a theme park, except with an office job."

"How did you pass for a paranormal?" Bolan asked.

"I hired a wizard to make me look like an elf. Legolas was my favorite *Lord of the Rings* character. I figured pointy ears would be a simple fix and help me blend in."

"Witches and wizards look human," Bolan pointed out.

"Yeah, but they have magic. I can't fake that, not easily anyway. And I didn't want to be short and green."

Bolan opened his mouth to comment, so I jumped in, "A wizard transformed your ears and then the mirror spell changed them back?"

Tyler sighed. "Everything was going great until that

spell happened. Now every time I look in the mirror, I have a mild panic attack until I remember that everybody looks different right now."

"It's how you view yourself," I explained. "You only want to appear as an elf to stay in town, not because you actually see yourself as a paranormal being."

He pressed his lips together, thinking. "Yeah. That makes sense," he finally said.

Bolan eyed him closely. "Did Bertram know the truth?"

Tyler balked. "Why would you ask that?"

"Because then you'd have a motive to kill him."

Tyler exhaled in exasperation. "I didn't kill him. He didn't know the truth about me, and even if he did, he wouldn't have ratted me out. Like you said, he treated me like one of his own sons."

"I'm sure his actual sons loved that," I remarked.

Tyler shrugged. "They're okay. Timothy's a mess, but Jeremiah has always seemed cool with it. He's the one who invited me to the birthday dinner. Timothy never would've thought to include me. Then again, Timothy couldn't plan his way out of a paper bag."

"That tracks," Bolan murmured.

"The wizard you mentioned," I began, "the one who performed the spell on you. Who was it?"

Tyler flinched. "I'm not allowed to say."

"Not allowed?" Bolan repeated. "Need I remind you that you're speaking to the sheriff's deputy?" He tapped his badge.

I had to admit, I appreciated Bolan's new swagger now that he was less green and less horizontally challenged. He reminded me more of Granger.

"I signed an NDA. I don't want to get sued."

"The wizard can't sue you if you reveal information as

part of a criminal investigation," I said. "There are always exceptions in contracts about that sort of thing." I hoped.

Tyler seemed to mull over my response.

"If you tell us, we promise to keep it confidential," Bolan added.

"You mean you won't speak to him?" Tyler asked hopefully.

"Oh, we have to speak to him," Bolan said, "but we'll make sure the information stays on a need-to-know basis."

Tyler hesitated. "If it might help catch Bert's killer, then I guess I should tell you. Bert would do the same for me." His jaw set. "But if I tell you, I want immunity."

Bolan frowned. "Immunity from prosecution?"

"From getting booted from Starry Hollow. I don't want you to come after me for being human."

I looked sideways at Bolan. I wasn't sure what the rules and regulations had to say about a case like this.

"Consider it done," Bolan said.

"The wizard's name is Evan Winter-Weaver."

"Thanks." I didn't recognize the name. It was possible he was another outcast like Olga. How many expelled coven members were there in Starry Hollow? Why not leave town?

"I'll leave the wizard to you," Bolan said. "Seems like more of a lead for the spell than the murder."

"I'll let you know what I find out."

Tyler glanced from Bolan to me. "That's it then? I get to stay in Starry Hollow?"

"That was the deal," I said.

Closing his eyes, Tyler blew out a long breath. "Thank you. You have no idea how much it means to me to stay here."

"I actually do, Tyler," I said. "More than you know."

Chapter Nine

Evan Winter-Weaver wasn't as easy to locate as I expected. I thought the coven would keep tabs on wizards they'd expelled, but Aster was surprised to learn he lived locally.

"I'm surprised he'd stay after all that," Aster had remarked, which left me wondering what "after all that" meant. I didn't get the chance to pursue it because Aspen decided that was the perfect moment to knock the good vase on the floor with the handle of a broomstick, and Aster hung up.

"I could try a locator spell," I said to PP3, except now I thought it would be prudent to find out more about Evan before I questioned him. If there was a chance he was dangerous, I'd rather be prepared.

Linnea was too preoccupied with her condition to answer the phone, and she was usually less informed than Aster when it came to coven business anyway. I didn't want to ask Aunt Hyacinth because that meant having a conversation with her. After the failure of the coven's counterspell, I figured her mood would be like dying your eyebrows to match your hair—best avoided.

I decided to visit the one place I could rely on for information. Delphine Winter was alone when I arrived at the library. I tried to picture the way she actually looked, instead of the hideous hag that greeted me.

"No research team assembled today?"

The not-so-pretty witch smiled at me, revealing a set of yellowed teeth. "We've been advised to stand down until further notice. I think your aunt is nursing a bruised ego." She splayed her hands on the counter, and I tried to ignore the yellowed fingernails. "Why? Did you come to help?"

"No, I came for something else."

She cast a furtive glance around the library and lowered her voice. "The book you requested isn't in yet. Apparently, it's very hard to get."

"I'm not here for the book." My cheeks grew warm. I'd finally decided to read *Fifty Shades of Grey* to see what all the fuss was about, but the library had to acquire a copy from their contacts in the human world. "What can you tell me about Evan Winter-Weaver?"

Delphine's eyebrows lifted almost imperceptibly. "He's my cousin."

"Oh, of course." Some investigator I was. I hadn't even made the connection.

"What do you want to know?"

"Why was he expelled from the coven?"

She kept her voice quiet. "Technically, he wasn't expelled. He left voluntarily, but he would've been forced out if he hadn't agreed to leave."

"What happened?"

She compressed her lips. "Let's go to the quiet room where we won't be overheard."

I followed her to the empty room adjacent to the lobby, and she closed the door behind us with a gentle click.

"Is the story that bad?" I asked.

Delphine made herself comfortable on a recliner and pulled a fuzzy blanket over her. "I just wanted an excuse to get cozy. All I need now is a cup of peppermint tea, and I'm happy."

"I'll bring you one next time. What's the deal with Evan? I need to speak to him about the mirror spell."

Delphine smoothed the fluffy blanket. "I'd be surprised if Evan had a hand in it after what he did."

The vagueness was wearing on me. "What did he do?" I demanded.

"It was an upsetting time for the coven. Natalie's such a sweetheart."

I perched on the arm of the leather sofa. "Who's Natalie?"

"Evan and Natalie were best friends, but it was obvious to everyone that he was in love with her. You couldn't look at them together without seeing it." Delphine smiled, and I wish she hadn't. It was hard enough to ignore the giant wart on her nose. Her teeth were next-level ugly.

"It was really sweet," Delphine continued. "They did everything together. Rode broomsticks, practiced spells. Evan was better than Natalie, and you could tell he wanted her skills to be as sharp as his."

"But he messed up?" I asked.

"Well, Natalie ended up in a coma, so I'd say yes."

"How long was she in the coma?"

"Two months. She made a full recovery, but the damage was done. By the time she woke up, Evan had left the coven, and her parents forbade her from contacting him." She paused. "It was actually your aunt who convinced the sheriff not to arrest Evan. Natalie's parents wanted him to pay, whatever that means."

"Aunt Hyacinth put her neck out for somebody? Why?" In my experience, she only acted in her own self-interest. If she wanted to keep Evan out of custody, she had a personal reason.

Delphine shrugged. "I always assumed it was to protect the coven. If Evan got arrested, word would spread that the coven wasn't safe. Or something like that."

That made more sense. "I don't think I've met Natalie. Does she come to the monthly meetings?"

"No, she tends to avoid coven gatherings. No one gives her a hard time because of the incident."

"Where does she live?"

Delphine rattled off the address. "She still lives with her parents. I heard they've become overly protective. It wouldn't surprise me if she lived with them until they died."

Poor Natalie. It sounded like she'd been through the wringer.

"Do you know where Evan lives?"

"My family said he's been spotted in the woods near Rueben Slate's abandoned cabin, but I don't know if that's just a rumor to scare kids. *Don't go into the woods or the Winter-Weaver will put you in a coma.* That sort of thing."

"You don't ask about him at family gatherings?"

"He's not exactly the prodigal son. Even before the incident, he was considered a little bit off. I liked to disappear into my books, but I knew when to be sociable and polite. Evan didn't seem to care what anybody else thought. He was openly antisocial."

"Except with Natalie."

"Except with Natalie." She smiled again, and my stomach turned.

It seemed to me that it might be worth speaking to Natalie first. If there was something important to know about Evan, she'd be in the best position to tell me.

"I guess you're really anxious to break this spell, huh?"

Delphine gave me a blank look. "Sure, I guess so." She didn't seem particularly eager.

"That wart doesn't bother you?" I pointed to her nose.

"It's been there my whole life. Why would it bother me now?"

I struggled for a polite reply. In the end, I gave up. "Are you insane? You don't have a wart like that anywhere on your body."

"Of course I do. This was the very first wart I ever got." She flicked the tip of her nose.

"Delphine, in real life that wart must be the size of a pinprick. You've magnified it in your mind." It pained me that she saw herself in such unattractive terms. "And your teeth…" I didn't know where to start. "What does Wren say?"

"That I'm still the most beautiful witch he's ever laid eyes on."

That's how you know you've got the right partner. Good for Wren. Even better for Delphine.

Natalie's house was in a typical suburban neighborhood. The houses and their lots were a little larger than average, suggesting higher income families, but there were very few trees. It seemed they'd mostly been cleared away to make space for the sprawling homes. Natalie's house was almost indistinguishable from those surrounding it. There must've been HOA rules in place because there was nary a garden gnome or personal decoration in sight. The only unique item I spotted was a cement pineapple by the front door. Pineapples were a sign of hospitality, so I took it as a good omen and knocked on the door.

A young woman answered. Her brown hair was styled in two braids, and she wore a collared shirt with a knee-length skirt. Her feet were bare.

"May I help you?" she asked. "My parents are at work, so if you're selling something, you'll have to come back."

"My name is Ember Rose. I was hoping to speak to Natalie."

"Rose," she repeated. "Are you related to the Rose-Muldoons?"

"Hyacinth is my aunt."

Natalie gasped. "You're her. You're the one who was raised in the human world."

I plastered on a smile. "That's me. I'm Starry Hollow famous."

"You really are." She widened the gap in the doorway. "Where are my manners? Please come in."

I stepped inside the grand foyer. The black-and-white checkerboard floor and multitiered chandelier seemed over the top for the stucco house, but who was I to judge? Everything seemed excessive to someone who once lived in a shabby, shoebox apartment with 70s decor.

"Why are you here to see *me*?" Natalie asked, as though the queen had deigned to pay her a royal visit.

"I have questions about an old friend of yours. Evan Winter-Weaver."

Her face grew pinched. "I'm sure you know the story. I'm not sure why you'd need to ask me any questions about it."

"And I'm sure you're aware of the spell that was cast on the town."

She nodded. "My parents can talk of little else. I'd like to undo the spell myself if only to change the dinner conversation."

I smiled. "Trust me. We're working on it."

"My mother said the coven had a failed attempt."

"Were they there?"

"No. They were both working late. Their jobs are very demanding."

"What do they do?"

"Lawyers." She motioned to the kitchen. "Want to sample my pumpkin bread? I just made a fresh loaf."

"Important question," I said. "Does it have chocolate chips?"

"Do I look like a monster to you? Of course it does."

I entered the kitchen behind her. The room was every bit as grand as one would've guessed from the foyer. I mean, the interior paled in comparison to Thornhold, but most houses did.

While Natalie sliced the bread, I made myself at home on a stool at the counter. "Tell me about your relationship with Evan."

She sighed deeply, as though the topic was a difficult one, which made sense. "We were best friends. We met in preschool and hit it off. He was the little boy eating paste that nobody wanted to play with."

"And that appealed to you?"

"He wasn't eating it because he was weird." She paused. "Okay, I guess it's still weird, but he was trying to decide whether he could develop a paste that tasted both good and wasn't toxic."

"Then it wouldn't be paste. It would be food."

She laughed. "Evan's mind was always going. He liked to think outside the box without judgment, and then rein in the thoughts afterward. He was later diagnosed with ADHD, but he refused to take any potions for it. He didn't want to quash his creativity."

"What did your parents think of your friendship?"

My question elicited a strong eye roll. "They prefer the right sort, if you know what I mean. Someone who can pass at a social function, make small talk without inducing a grimace. They became lawyers for a reason."

Her parents were probably friends with Aunt Hyacinth. "And that wasn't Evan, I take it."

She laughed. "Definitely not. He was a black sheep from the start."

"Did your parents ever interfere?"

"They never took steps to cut us off. Their approach was stealthier. They'd try to steer me toward others they felt were more acceptable. They'd arrange play dates with the children of other lawyers from their firm."

"But Evan was still in the mix?"

Her head bobbed. "He and I had a connection. I can't explain it. Don't really feel the need to. It wasn't romantic, not that my parents believed me. I think they were secretly terrified I'd marry him someday."

I wasn't sure I believed her either. Her tone of voice carried a reverent quality when she spoke of him. I wondered whether she was aware of it. Probably not. "And then the coma happened."

Natalie's demeanor changed. The light faded from her eyes, and her mouth turned down at the corners. "It was a difficult time for everybody. I almost feel like the lucky one because I was unconscious for the hardest part."

"Can you tell me what happened?"

"Why do we need to rehash it? The past is best left in the past. Great Goddess of the Moon." Her eyes grew large and round, and she clamped a hand over her mouth. "Is this about the spell? Do you think Evan's responsible?"

I saw no reason to lie. "He's on the list of options."

She inhaled sharply. "It hadn't occurred to me."

"Why not?"

"Because he ... I would've thought he learned his lesson."

"You're not in touch with him now?"

Averting her gaze, she slid the plate of pumpkin bread across the counter to me. "It seemed best to cut ties. He carried around a lot of guilt. My parents carried blame." She trailed off. "There was too much conflict, and I'm not great at handling conflict."

"What about you, though? How do you feel about the situation?"

"I don't feel much of anything." She gave an awkward laugh. "I understand why everyone thinks it's best that we don't spend time together anymore."

It sounded to me like the decision had been forced upon her rather than chosen by her. Time to dig a little deeper. "What else can you tell me about Evan? Does he have a temper?"

"A temper?" She burst into laughter. "Gods, no. If Evan felt angry, he'd want to know why. Then his anger would subside while he conducted an internal investigation."

"So you think he still has that same natural curiosity from childhood?"

"One hundred percent. He made me think about topics I never would've considered. It wouldn't occur to me to wonder why a starfish grows back its limb, but his insatiable curiosity was infectious. I'd start thinking more about subjects I previously would've glossed over."

"He sounds like a good wizard to know." A shame her

parents saw things differently. It seemed Evan had a positive impact on their daughter, apart from the whole coma debacle.

"I wish him well. Truly." She nibbled on a slice of bread. "I hope he's thriving, whatever he's doing now."

"You really don't keep tabs on him?" Part of me wondered whether they'd kept in secret contact, but it didn't seem like it.

Natalie shook her head. "It would be too easy to fall back into old habits. No contact keeps that door firmly closed."

"I'm glad you made a full recovery."

"Not a *full* recovery," she replied with a trace of sadness. "Don't forget, I lost Evan."

Chapter Ten

Nobody seemed to know the whereabouts of Evan Winter-Weaver, so my only option was to check out the section of the woods with the abandoned cabin that Delphine had mentioned. Everybody seemed to know about the old Rueben Slate cabin except me. It served as a gentle reminder that I still didn't know everything there was to know about Starry Hollow.

Raoul insisted on accompanying me. I suspected he was more interested in scoping out a new woodland neighborhood than finding a wizard.

I smell wolves, Raoul said.

"Maybe they run through here at night."

He pointed to trampled bushes. *I think you're right.*

"Any sign of this cabin?"

Raoul stopped to pluck a berry off a bush. *You're here for the cabin. I'm here for the snacks.*

"Are you sure that's not poisonous?"

He licked the berry. *I like to live dangerously.*

"If you consider vomiting for the next five hours living dangerously, have at it."

He tossed the berry over his shoulder and continued his quest for nonthreatening treats.

Finally, we arrived at a large clearing. It took me a minute to process what I was seeing. The cabin in the woods wasn't the idyllic wooden structure I expected to find. Instead, the building was covered in colorful graffiti. At one end, dolphins swam over a glittery rainbow. A smiling green skeleton with curved horns had been painted over the top of the front door. Aside from the graffiti, the rest of the cabin seemed neat and tidy. A lone rocking chair sat out front with a stack of logs beside it. There was no garden to speak of, only the natural foliage found in this section of the forest.

This artwork is spectacular, Raoul declared. *Whoever did this is really talented.*

"I don't think it's done by one artist. The styles are too different."

Maybe they're different periods, like Picasso's blue period.

"Like the Sea World period and Skeletor period?"

Raoul ignored me. *Do you think he actually lives in the cabin? I thought it was supposed to be abandoned.*

"I don't know. Delphine said he's been spotted in the area, and the logs suggest somebody might be inside." I knocked on the front door. "You stay outside and look around."

For what?

"Clues," I said vaguely.

He leaned back to admire the graffiti directly in front of him. *I don't know that I'll get much done. I think this artwork might be spelled. I feel mesmerized looking at it.*

"I think the word you're looking for is dizzy." Or maybe nauseous.

The door creaked open, and a youthful wizard blinked at me from behind thick glasses.

"I'm sorry to bother you. Are you Evan Winter-Weaver?"

"Yes. Do you have my delivery?"

"No, I'm sorry. I'm not here with a delivery. I'm Ember Rose, private investigator." I held up my business card for inspection. Anyone who lived alone in the forest likely had a strong mistrust of strangers.

He frowned as he read the card. "Any relation to Hyacinth?"

"She's my aunt."

"I didn't realize she had a niece."

"I didn't realize I had an aunt until I moved here."

His gaze flicked over me. He seemed to be debating whether to close the door.

"I'm here to talk to you about Natalie," I said quickly. "I understand my aunt was instrumental in keeping you out of the system."

"Why do you need to talk to me? Natalie woke up years ago. Case closed, Madam Investigator."

"Okay, technically this isn't about Natalie. There's a situation that you might be able to help with."

He was visibly surprised. "You want *my* help?"

"Yes. Your cousin Delphine says you're very talented, or at least you were."

"Delphine," he said softly. "How is my cousin? I always liked her."

"She's great." Hideous at the moment, but that would hopefully change very soon.

"Where are my manners? You live alone in the woods long enough and you forget common courtesy. Come in. Don't mind the mess. I was working on my duck."

He said duck, right? Raoul's voice cut into my thoughts. *Please confirm before you go in there.*

I didn't need to ask for clarification. The moment I entered the cabin, I saw the evidence. Along the floor was a neat row of wooden ducks. Each one was painted with a different color bill. Bright pink. Orange. Green. Blue. The ducks were nearly identical apart from the color of the bill.

He carves wooden ducks, I told the raccoon.

Phew.

"These are great," I said, motioning to the ducks. "Is this your hobby?"

"No, I sell them online. They're very popular. For extra money, I'll add a collar with a name." He pointed to the wooden duck on the mantel with a shiny purple bill. "That one's mine. It's the first one I ever made. I take it you're not here to talk about my duck, though."

He's still saying duck, right?

Go look for clues, I yelled in my head. "No, this has nothing to do with your work." The interior of the cabin was much homier than outside. "I never would've guessed how nice it is in here."

"That's because I spelled the cabin's exterior to make it continue to look abandoned so no one would bother me." He wore a rueful smile. "Big mistake. Local teens started coming out here to party. They'd bring plenty of spray paint."

"They didn't break in?"

"They would have if I hadn't warded it to keep them out."

"Why not ward the property line to keep them from getting close enough to paint the cabin?"

"That was my next move, but I decided I liked the artwork. The next time they showed up at night, I brought them hot cocoa and introduced myself. I told them they were welcome to keep adding to the murals, but to keep it clean and please respect my privacy."

"That's one way of handling it."

Evan shrugged. "I was once a young teenager with nowhere productive to channel my energy. I understand them."

I motioned to the ducks. "You seem able to keep your ducks in a row now. Pun intended."

"It took me many years to find something that helped me maintain my focus."

I remembered his refusal to take a potion for his attention condition. "How did you settle on carving ducks?"

"I like to take morning walks in the woods. There's a pond about half a mile from here where the ducks gather. I started to picture them with bright colors like the murals. I didn't want the whole duck to be painted, so I experimented with only the bill."

"I'm glad it worked out for you."

"I still dabble in magic because it pays better and puts food on my plate, but the ducks feed my soul." He smiled at me. "You must have something that keeps your soul afloat, Ms. Rose."

I fumbled for an answer. "I have my relationships. My daughter and my loved ones."

"Those are external sources," Evan said. "I'm talking about what comes from within." He tapped his chest.

"I've never been particularly creative." That was Marley's domain. Her artistic talents never ceased to amaze me.

"It doesn't need to be a creative pursuit. It could be any activity that fills your spiritual well."

"I'll have to get back to you on that one." I was too busy

with everyday tasks to worry about "keeping my soul afloat." It was more like keeping my bills from sinking us. "Were you impacted by the mirror spell?"

"No, although I heard about it from two of the teens that regularly come around. One of them had a face covered in zits, all with pus." Evan shuddered. "Seems like a horrible spell."

"Depends on who you ask. Why do you think you weren't affected?" It could be that Evan was one of the lucky ones where his outside already matched his inside.

"It's probably because of the anti-magic ward around the cabin," he replied.

"What kind of ward?"

"I didn't want retaliation for what happened to Natalie, so I put up a ward that protects me from outside magic."

Then again, maybe he wasn't affected because he cast the spell in the first place.

"How long ago was that?"

He stroked his chin in a thoughtful gesture. "Maybe two years ago, but I have to boost it every now and then or it gets too weak."

"Do you still worry about retaliation?" It seemed unlikely given that Natalie was fine, and nobody talked about the incident anymore. Nobody even knew where to find Evan.

"It's possible I'm being paranoid. I just remember the look in her mother's eye." Evan cringed. "If she could've killed me right there and then without repercussions, I think she would have."

I understood a mother's fury.

He lifted up his glasses and rubbed the bridge of his nose. "Is the mirror spell the reason you're here? Do you want to ask about how someone might've accomplished it?"

"Honestly, I wanted to ask whether *you* might've accomplished it."

Evan looked taken aback. "Me? Absolutely not. I'm very selective about the magic I practice nowadays. I wouldn't dream of taking such a huge risk."

"Any thoughts on how to undo it? The coven tried, but it didn't work."

"The whole coven? How curious. Who could be that powerful as to resist the counterspell of an entire coven?"

"I think it's more than power. I suspect we're missing a key piece of information, like maybe it was designed to only be undone by the caster."

"Or the spell was an accident. It's harder to piece together a counterspell for one that wasn't done with intention in the first place." He grimaced. "Ask me how I know."

I gave him a long look. It seemed to me that Evan had suffered enough. "Maybe you should talk to Natalie's parents. Try to smooth over the bumps."

He shook his head emphatically. "They don't want anything to do with me."

"It might put your fears to rest. Request a meeting over coffee. Offer a final apology and tell them you're happy that Natalie's alive and well, and that you hope you can all leave the past behind you."

Evan seemed to mull over the suggestion. "It's not a bad idea. It might help with the nightmares."

"You still have nightmares about it?"

He rubbed the back of his neck. "I don't really like to talk about them. It's one of the reasons I only use magic on a limited basis. I worry about making another mistake that ends in tragedy."

"If you don't mind me asking, what went wrong with the spell that injured Natalie?"

"I was distracted by her ... existence. She'd curled her hair for a party later that night. She looked so pretty." His expression turned wistful. "I wasn't paying close enough attention to the spell."

Poor Evan. He'd been so lovestruck that he nearly killed the object of his affection with a spell. He probably didn't trust himself.

"You know, sometimes saying horrible things out loud helps break their hold on you. If you talk to someone about the nightmares, they might stop." Or if you go to the source of them...

Evan offered a vague smile. "Well, this was an unexpected development. Thank you for stopping by. I'm sorry I couldn't help with the mirror spell."

Raoul's voice interrupted my response. *I found a greenhouse. It's camouflaged, but I could smell the herbs.*

I cleared my throat. "One last question before I go. Why do you have a secret greenhouse?"

He winced. "You found that, did you? It's hidden so the locals don't raid it. There's nothing illegal in there, I swear."

"May I see?"

"You don't believe me?"

I shrugged. "Trust but verify."

He sighed. "Very well. I'll put *your* fears to rest."

We exited the cabin, and I followed him to a trail behind the cabin where I saw Raoul pacing near a smaller clearing.

"Your partner, I presume?" Evan asked, inclining his head toward the raccoon.

"My familiar, Raoul."

Evan waved a hand and the greenhouse appeared. It was pretty basic. He wasn't lying about the contents either. The herbs were all aboveboard. Nothing poisonous.

"I'd let the locals paint murals on the greenhouse, except then they'd know about it," he admitted.

"Can't you ward it to keep them from entering and still let them paint the outside?"

He pondered the structure. "I suppose. Then again, I like that it's my little oasis that nobody knows about. Even when I have clients meet me at the cabin, I don't show them where I keep the spell ingredients."

I took a closer look at the pots. There was nothing here powerful enough to conjure the kind of massive spell that impacted everyone in town. I was coming to accept that Evan didn't have the skills or the inclination to cast the mirror spell.

"Just out of curiosity, if someone had offered you a good chunk of change to cast a spell on Starry Hollow, would you have done it?"

Evan recoiled. "Gods, no. After what I did to Natalie, I'd never take on that level of risk. Even now, I'll refuse a request if I think there's a chance of negative consequences."

It didn't surprise me that Evan had developed scruples after putting someone in a coma. He'd have to be a sociopath to carry on as though nothing had happened.

Against my better judgment, I decided to wade into personal waters. "You must miss Natalie. It sounds like you two had a wonderful friendship."

His head drooped. "The best. She was the Watson to my Holmes. The Mindy to my Mork."

What's a Mork? Raoul asked.

"Would you consider a reconciliation with her? Maybe reestablish a friendship."

"I think about it all the time." His face grew pained. "I still miss her every day. She was my best friend. Half of the ducks I've painted have green bills because that was her favorite color."

"You wanted more than friendship." It was more of a statement than a question. It was obvious to anybody with their senses intact that they were in love with each other.

He swallowed hard. "It doesn't matter what I want."

"Of course it does. You deserve love as much as anybody else."

"After what I did?" He shook his head. "I deserve to be alone in the woods until I die. Just me and my..."

Raoul covered his ears. *Duck, right? Quack quack.*

I shot the raccoon a silencing glance. "You know, Evan, I spoke with Natalie recently. For what it's worth, she spoke very highly of you and doesn't seem to harbor any ill will. I don't think she'd be opposed to hearing from you if you felt brave enough to contact her."

His eyebrows drew together. "Really? What did she say?"

"It was what she didn't say that spoke volumes. She misses you, Evan. I'm sure if you reached out to her, she'd be open to it. Her parents work a lot, so I bet if you went to the house during office hours, you wouldn't have to worry about a run-in with them."

He took a moment to digest that bombshell. "Natalie misses me," he murmured. "Could she still care about me after what I did?"

"You're both still young," I said. "You can make up for lost time."

"What if her parents disapprove?"

"I said you're young, not children. If the relationship is worth it to her, then she'll do whatever it takes to make it happen."

Evan appeared doubtful. "Then why hasn't she reached

out to me all this time? She's the reason I never left town. I knew if I did, she'd be lost to me forever."

My chest ached. He'd remained in Starry Hollow in a dingy cabin in the woods out of hope. Poor wizard. He truly loved her.

Evan eyed me closely. "You must not think I'm guilty of casting the spell if you're encouraging me to pursue Natalie."

"I have a gut instinct that says you're on the level."

"It's the ducks, isn't it?" He grinned. "They're charming."

"They really are." I glanced in the direction of the wooden ducks. "In fact, I wouldn't mind taking one home for my daughter if you've got one available. I think she'd get a kick out of it."

Evan gave a rueful shake of his head. "I'm sorry, Ms. Rose, but right now I have zero ducks to give."

Chapter Eleven

I dropped off Raoul at the cottage and continued to Granger's place to update him on the case. The door was unlocked, and I let myself in. I found the wolf curled up on the sofa, looking pathetic. I flopped beside him and stroked his soft fur.

"You're miserable, I know. I'm so sorry. I wish I could wave a magic wand and turn you back." In fact, I'd already tried that but to no avail.

Granger licked my hand.

"Have you eaten? I bet you're hungry."

He whined softly, and guilt swept over me. I should've been more attentive to him. My boyfriend needed me, and I'd completely dropped the ball—and not to play fetch.

"Let's get you fed." I walked into the kitchen, feeling oddly domestic as I prepared a meal for my wolf boyfriend. I opened a package of raw steak and slid the meat onto a plate. Not wanting it to look too plain, I rifled through the spice rack until I found the paprika. "There. That'll add an extra bit of flavor."

I turned to the wolf. "Would you prefer the table or the floor?"

He jumped onto a chair, so I placed the plate on the table in front of him. While he ate, I updated him on the case. Every so often his ear would twitch, and I'd tug that thread, talking through what I'd learned until he seemed satisfied. When I mentioned Carly Santana for a third time, he barked.

"Bolan already spoke to her without me and thinks she's a dead end." Carly Santana was at the dinner party and had been the object of the dead fairy's affection. According to Bolan, she didn't see what happened to the victim either and was still reeling from the event.

Granger barked again.

"Fine. If you think it's worth another conversation, I'm happy to go. Who wants to visit a witness with me?" I asked in my best "good boy" voice.

The wolf growled.

"Sorry, I can't help it. I'll try to use my normal voice." I cleared my throat. "Would you like to pay a visit to Carly with me?"

The wolf nodded.

"Please don't be offended, but do you want to wear a collar? Then we can attach your sheriff badge. Make you look more official."

The wolf raised his head and looked at me with a deadpan expression.

I wagged a finger at him. "You promised you wouldn't be offended. Okay, you didn't promise, but I'm only trying to help establish your authority. Carly might be more willing to talk if she realizes it's the sheriff asking."

The wolf glanced in the direction of the bedroom.

"Got it. I'll look for it in there." I hurried into his

bedroom and opened the top drawer of the bedside table. For a brief moment, I was worried I'd find something I didn't want to see there, like a book by Mitch Albom. The reality was much worse.

My heart pounded as I stared at the velvet ring box.

It wasn't worse in the sense that I didn't want to marry him—I truly did. It was just that now I knew there was a ring inside that box, and all I had to do was open it to see what the ring looked like. What if it was ugly? I contemplated that thought further. How ugly could an engagement ring really be? I then made the mistake of doing a quick internet search for 'ugly engagement rings.'

Sweet baby Elvis. It could be *real* ugly.

I shut the drawer. Nope. Not gonna look. I loved Granger Nash with all my heart and whatever he chose for me would be a perfect token of his love. A plastic ring from a vending machine would suit me fine, preferably a candy ring that allowed me to eat the sugary 'gemstone.'

I continued to linger in front of the drawer, unable to move. One quick peek could confirm my belief.

Or it could destroy it.

I took a step backward. "Walk away, Ember," I told myself. "Have a little faith in the man you love."

Unless the spell was broken soon, there'd be plenty of time before he'd be able to propose anyway. He wouldn't want to salivate during one of the most romantic moments of his life.

I spotted the collar hanging on a hook on the closet door and snagged it. Heart pounding, I fled the bedroom and found Granger licking the bottom of his plate. All done.

"Now you'll have plenty of energy for an interview." I fastened the collar around his thick neck and affixed his badge to the black material. I ran my fingers through the fur on his back.

"I miss the less hairy version of your back," I told him.

He whimpered softly.

I wrapped my arms around him and squeezed. "We're burning the candles at both ends to get this case solved and the spell broken. I'm not sure what else we can do that we're not already doing."

His body was so warm and soft. I wouldn't have objected to curling up on the sofa together and taking a well-deserved nap.

I kissed the top of his head. "Time to go. Let me do the talking," I teased.

He jumped to the floor and waited for me to open the door. I knew he hated every second of this, having to rely on someone else. I understood because I hated it too. We both liked our independence, although I think it had been forced on both of us before we were ready. It was one of the reasons we appreciated each other so much. He seemed to sense when I needed him to step forward and when I needed him to step back. I felt like I'd failed him today, leaving him to fend for himself too long. I wouldn't make that mistake again.

I closed the door behind us and locked it. I was here now, and I wouldn't let him down again.

I rolled down the window so Granger could hang his head outside on the way to Carly Santana's house. He seemed happier now that he was able to burn off some energy. It must've been hard for him to be cooped up indoors. It was against his nature even in his human form.

"Want me to throw you a ball at the beach afterward?" I offered.

The wolf glowered at me.

"Just asking."

Carly's house was a sweet bungalow painted pale blue with white trim and shutters. The front porch was cluttered with handmade items, like a wooden topiary painted with red and pink hearts and a set of rustic chairs that showed off the natural grain of the wood. I hadn't even met Carly yet, but I could already envision the type of woman she was.

"I bet she gives the best hugs," I told Granger as we stood on the front porch.

He sniffed the crafts, and I waited until he returned to my side to knock on the door.

The moment I saw Carly, I understood why two grown paranormals had been clamoring for her attention. Her white hair shimmered like freshly fallen snow, and her skin seemed to defy gravity. I was tempted to find an old photo of her so I could determine whether her appearance was real or the effect of the spell.

"Carly Santana, I'm Ember Rose, and this is Sheriff Nash." I inclined my head toward the wolf. "I know you've already spoken with Deputy Bolan, but we'd like a few more minutes of your time, if you don't mind."

Carly smiled at the wolf. "It's a pleasure to meet you, Sheriff. I heard you were out of commission."

Granger's ears twitched.

"He's involved in the case, but obviously, his participation is somewhat limited," I explained.

"Won't you come in?" Carly gestured to the interior. "I have a comfortable spot for the sheriff to rest."

I spotted the comfortable spot as soon as I entered the

house. It was an oversized dog bed tucked in the corner of the room. It looked insanely cozy.

"Where's your dog?" I asked, suddenly aware of a potential conflict between the animals.

"Clark died last year, but I haven't been able to convince myself to get rid of the bed." Carly sighed. "I like having a few reminders of him around. It still smells like him."

"What kind of dog was he?"

Carly lifted a framed photo from the end table and handed it to me. It showed Carly kneeling beside a blue-eyed husky.

"He was gorgeous," I said. And so was Carly. The mirror spell didn't seem to have changed her in any obvious way.

She sighed. "He was. Such a wonderful companion. It was after he died that I decided to start dating again. I'd given up on it for years after a string of bad relationships."

"And then you met two good ones." I cut myself off, not sure whether I should've revealed how much I knew about her relationships.

"I did." Smiling, Carly plucked the photo from my hand and placed it back on the end table. "Can I offer you a refreshment? I have homemade burstberry tea. I drink it iced, but I can warm it for you. I also made gingerbread cookies with icing in honor of Bert. They were his favorite."

I turned to the wolf. "Anything for you?"

To my relief, Granger crossed the room and settled on the bed. I suspected he was doing it to be polite. Gods above, he was able to show compassion even in his wolf form.

"I would love an iced tea and a cookie," I said. It would

ruin my next meal, but it wasn't as though I had a dinner plan. I'd wing it, as usual.

As I followed Carly to the small but well-equipped kitchen, I noticed all the knickknacks. They seemed to fill every shelf and crevice in the house.

"You're very crafty," I remarked.

"I'm a retired teacher," she said. "Comes with the territory."

"Oh, which school?"

"The local elementary. I was more than ready to hang up my smock." She smiled. "The parents were more tiring than the children, to be honest."

"That's what I hear." As a so-called broomstick mama, you would think I'd fall into that category, but school was one of the areas where I kept my distance unless absolutely necessary.

Carly poured two glasses of iced burstberry tea.

"I'm sorry about Bertram," I said. "I understand you two were close."

Her expression clouded over as she opened the container of gingerbread cookies. "His birthday started out on such a high. I still can't believe how it ended."

"It must have been difficult for you to be right there when he died." I bit into the cookie and immediately tasted the spices and molasses. It took all my willpower not to moan.

"I was at the party," Carly began, "but I missed his ... final moments. As soon as the spell hit, I ran."

That seemed to be the common reaction, which was strange because nobody at Thornhold moved a muscle. Then again, nobody ran in Aunt Hyacinth's house without the risk of ejection.

"Why did you run?"

"I was embarrassed." She lifted a foot, and it was then that I noticed the size of her orange flip-flop. "I can't even wear proper shoes at the moment."

"Your feet aren't usually this large, I take it?"

"No, but I've always worried about my feet. They grew before the rest of me, so I've had this insecurity around their size since I was twelve. My brother used to tease me and call me a hobbit."

"And now the mirror spell has made the internal external."

She released a small sigh. "I know it could be worse; they could be hairy too."

I nodded toward Granger who'd wandered into the kitchen. "Some are definitely hairier than others."

She gave the sheriff a sympathetic smile. "I realize it's not as bad as others have it, but it's still keeping me up at night." She looked down at her feet. "I realize now how silly I've been all these years to think my feet were too big. I hope the spell is broken soon, so I can appreciate the feet I actually have."

I pivoted to Granger. "Cookie?"

He panted, and I tossed him a gingerbread man. He opened his massive jaws and swallowed it whole.

"Tell me about your relationship with Bertram," I said to Carly.

Her smile turned sad. "He was wonderful. Treated me with kindness and respect. Seventy is far too soon to lose him."

I slurped the tea, which was every bit as delicious as the cookie. Carly was the whole package. I didn't blame Bertram and Eugene for their shared interest in her.

"Bert and I could talk for hours," she said wistfully. "He was a good listener, a rare quality in a man, let me tell you." She cut a glance at Granger. "No offense, Sheriff."

The wolf barked.

"What kind of things did you talk about?"

She leaned against the counter, thinking. "I think we covered every topic we could think of. Childhood. Philosophy. Politics. Education, of course. Favorite songs." She paused. "His was a human song, *Fly Me to the Moon*. Do you know it?"

"Frank Sinatra." Another New Jerseyan.

Her smile brightened her whole face. "That's the one. He would sing it whenever he was in a good mood."

"Was that often?"

She nodded. "Bert was always in good spirits. He did worry on occasion, though."

"About what?"

"The usual things. His boys. Timothy, in particular."

I smiled. "I had the pleasure of meeting Timothy."

She stifled a laugh. "He's not so bad, but I understand why Bert worried. It can't be easy when you have a son like Jeremiah. You can't help but compare and wonder where you went wrong. I met plenty of parents over the years who struggled with the same thing. They'd have their older child mastering every skill with ease, and then the second one comes along and can't seem to cut with scissors or sit still for more than thirty seconds at a time."

"I understand. I have an aunt who worries where she went wrong with each one of her children. No comparison required."

Carly laughed. "She would fit right in with the parents of my former students. I've considered writing a book to educate parents on those early years. As far as I was concerned, they tended to focus on the wrong things."

"Like what?" I prompted.

"Oh, you know. They'd fret if little William earned only a satisfactory in mathematics and wanted to know how he could earn extra credit." She gave a rueful shake of her head. "William was six. I'd much rather focus on the fact that William was kind and showed compassion to his fellow students."

"Can't they focus on both?"

"Sure, except that isn't what happens. They become fixated on the thing that matters the least. Before you know it, little William hates math, has internalized that he's "bad" at it, and he's set on a path that maybe wasn't the right one for him. Given time, maybe William's brain would've caught up to math at a more advanced level. It happens all the time."

"Do you think Bertram was guilty of that with his sons?"

Carly looked thoughtful. "I suppose so. He said his wife especially liked to coddle Timothy because he was born premature. I was constantly telling Bert to relax and not give Timothy's decisions too much attention, unless he was truly hurting himself, which he wasn't. Timothy is still young and figuring out his life. It had to be difficult for him to lose his mom when she doted on him as much as she did."

"Jeremiah and Timothy are hardly adolescents."

She sniffed. "Spoken like a true young woman. I'm sure everybody seems old from where you're standing. It's all a matter of perspective."

I was suddenly dying to ask Carly her age, but I didn't dare risk it. Not with feet her size.

"Is that what you told nervous parents? To alter their perspectives?"

"Pretty much." She looked me up and down. "You don't

strike me as a parent that would've demanded a sit-down in my classroom."

"No, I wasn't overly involved. That being said, I've been fortunate that my daughter has always been a model student." And school didn't interest me when Marley was younger. My interest in learning didn't truly kick in until I moved to Starry Hollow and, even then, it depended on the subject. Runes would never make their way into the mental bucket I wanted to fill. Sorry, Hazel.

"What can you tell me about Bertram's other friends and family members?"

"He was beloved by all of them," Carly said.

"And what about Eugene?"

She flinched. "What about him?"

"Did your relationship with him impact his friendship with Bertram?"

Her face darkened. "I didn't pit them against each other, if that's what you're really asking."

"It isn't. I'm simply asking about Bertram's best friend."

"I know their relations were strained for a bit, but they seemed to come around. I told them if they didn't patch things up that I'd walk away from both of them. I had no desire to be some femme fatale that breaks up longstanding friendships. It's one of the reasons I couldn't bring myself to choose one over the other. I knew it would mark the end of our trio."

"They persuaded you to stick around."

"I couldn't resist, honestly. I adored Bert," Carly said with a regretful sigh.

"What about Jeremiah and Timothy? How's your relationships with them?"

"I think they were worried about me," she said, "at least

Jeremiah was. It makes sense. He's the older, responsible one, and with his mother dead..."

"Timothy was closer to her, though."

"Oh, I know, but I get the sense Jeremiah had taken on a parental role, more so after his mom died. Bert and Timothy struggled, and they relied on Jeremiah to keep the family ticking along."

"That's a lot of weight on his shoulders."

"Bert confessed that he poured himself into his job and used it to avoid his emotions, which didn't serve the boys well. Then I came along, and I think Jeremiah was initially concerned I might be a gold digger. Bert had amassed a small fortune from working all those years, plus he'd inherited his wife's assets."

One look around Carly's house and you could tell she wasn't after anyone's money. She struck me as woman content. "I take it you eventually won over Jeremiah."

She flashed a smile. "I did. He's a typical firstborn. You just have to know how to appeal to him."

"Did you ever consider having kids of your own?"

"I wanted them." She patted her abdomen. "My body had other plans. The gods decided to grant them to me through the classroom."

"I'm so sorry. I shouldn't have presumed."

"It's okay. You wouldn't be the first, although I admit it's been many years since the topic came up."

I glanced at Granger. The wolf angled his head toward the door. It seemed he was satisfied with the conversation.

"I won't take up any more of your time," I said. "Thanks for the hospitality."

"I enjoyed the company," Carly replied. "Would you like to take home a few cookies for your daughter?"

"I wouldn't say no to that." I'd have to hide them from

Raoul, or they might disappear before Marley saw them. The raccoon was like a reverse Santa Claus.

Carly placed the cookies in a sealed bag and handed it to me. "I hope you figure out how to break the spell soon. I really miss wearing proper shoes." She glanced at the sheriff. "And I'm sure you do, too."

The wolf whined.

"He's saying he agrees," I translated.

"He's lucky to have someone who understands him so well," Carly said. "That's one thing I'll miss about Bert. He truly seemed to 'get' everyone, if you know what I mean."

"It's a talent," I agreed. Then again, if Bert were so adept at understanding everyone, how did he end up dead?

Chapter Twelve

Although Granger rode home with me, he immediately left the car and raced into the woods behind the cottage. I didn't take it personally. A wolf needed to do what a wolf needed to do.

I cobbled together a dinner of macaroni and cheese for Marley and was able to present her with the gingerbread cookies for dessert before Raoul made an appearance.

Marley's blue eyes widened as she chewed. "Did you make these? They're amazing."

"Sadly, I can't take credit." Although I was sorely tempted.

"We should bake more," Marley said. "I think we'd both enjoy it."

"I enjoy the eating. You can enjoy the baking."

"Maybe this weekend, if I don't have too much homework," she mused.

Her comment reminded me of my conversation with Evan and his remark about filling the well of my soul.

"You should bake anyway," I said. "You know you'll get your homework done. Ferris Bueller once said to slow down and enjoy life or you'll miss—or something to that effect."

Marley arched an eyebrow. "Okay," she said slowly. "Is this what the start of a midlife crisis looks like? Quoting '80s movies?"

"I'll pretend I didn't hear that." I exited the kitchen and walked to the closet. Inside, nestled in the corner, was my broomstick. As much as I loved to ride, I'd put the broomstick away because it had been a gift from Alec. It had been hard for me to enjoy something when the memories attached to it were so painful. Being with Granger was amazing, but it didn't erase my experience with Alec.

I seized the broomstick. It was time to move past the pain. I didn't want to cease an activity because of someone else. If I did, that meant Alec still had power over me. If I couldn't deal with the memories, then I could always sell the broomstick and buy myself a new one. But I shouldn't give up flying, not when it brought me joy.

I hefted the broomstick in my hand. There was no way I could afford one as nice as this. Alec had given it to me as a token of his love, so I tried to focus on those positive associations.

PP3 raised his head and gave me an appraising look as I walked past the sofa.

"I'm going out for a ride," I told the dog. "I won't be long."

Marley observed me from the kitchen doorway. "Do you want company?"

"No, thanks. This is me time."

"Phew, I was hoping you'd say that."

I smiled. "Still afraid of heights?"

"Not as much as before, but I still don't think flying will become a favorite pastime."

"Fair enough. You can bake, and I'll fly. See? We're not the same."

"There's nothing wrong with wanting to be like you," she insisted.

I left the cottage and stood outside, breathing in the cool night air. I took a moment to admire the starry sky. They didn't name this place Starry Hollow for nothing. Even if there'd been no moon, there were enough stars to light up the entire canvas above our heads. It seemed as though I could see every constellation in existence, which, of course, was impossible. Still, it was breathtaking to behold. Evan was right. It was important to take time for activities that were less about being productive and more about appreciating the sheer miracle of our existence. Fill that spiritual bucket.

I sat on the broomstick and launched myself into the air. The wind blew my hair straight back, and I cursed myself for not bringing a hair tie. Next time.

A night flight was as close to a religious experience as I could get. I flew over the Silver Moon headquarters, the academy, the athletic fields, the fountain, the Painted Pixies, the Lighthouse. I steered clear of the wharf where the broomsticks would be out in full force for a moonlight ride. I wasn't in the mood to mix with others. This ride demanded solitude.

Observing the town from a different vantage reminded me how fortunate I was to live here. Starry Hollow was such a stunning place, it seemed as though the love I felt for it was being reflected back to me.

I became aware of the rapid beating of my heart, and it pleased me to know I still found riding a broomstick as thrilling as ever. I needed to incorporate more opportunity for rides in my schedule. I prioritized work and other duties.

Partly it was out of habit—as a broke single mom in New Jersey, I didn't have the luxury of prioritizing anything else. But here, in Starry Hollow, I didn't have to do that anymore. Okay, money was a little tight at the moment, but the situation wasn't dire. I could afford to take thirty minutes to appreciate my life and enjoy it more than I did. I deserved it.

I skimmed the rooftop of Palmetto House and considered dropping by to check on tiny Linnea, but the sight of Wyatt's truck parked out front changed my mind. I'd let them argue in peace.

At Balefire Beach I turned left. The sound of the waves lapping gently against the shoreline sang me home. As I approached the woods behind Rose Cottage, I decided to fly through the trees to test my skills. I lowered my altitude and raced through the forest, tipping left and then right to dodge the woodland obstacles. Live oaks surrounded me as I flew toward the cottage. I pulled up the nose of the broomstick to avoid a stump and nearly collided with a thick branch. Up ahead a cobweb sparkled in a beam of moonlight. I narrowly missed destroying it. I shot straight through a thicket and felt the scratches on my arms and legs. They'd hurt tomorrow.

In the distance, I heard the howl of a wolf. Granger. I had to find a way to break this spell. I missed my boyfriend, and the sound of his lonely howl told me he felt the same.

I tilted left to pass another tree, and that's when I saw it in a clearing—the shadow. I flew past so quickly that I thought I might've imagined it. I craned my neck to look over my shoulder, but it was too late. The shadow was gone.

It wouldn't be that strange to see a shadow in the woods, even at this hour. Something about the image gave me pause, however. The silhouette seemed familiar somehow. I was tempted to turn around and fly back in search of it, but I'd already taken more time than I'd planned. I needed sleep more than I needed to investigate what was likely a projection of my imagination.

I exited the woods with leaves and twigs in my hair. I half expected to end up with a bird's nest as a hat. I landed out front and continued to sit for a moment, allowing the exhilaration to settle. My heart felt full.

Good trip? Raoul asked.

I turned to see the raccoon's shadow. "Why are you outside?"

The kitchen window was locked.

"I don't know who did that." As soon as the words were out of my mouth, I remembered that I was the culprit. I'd done it to prevent him from discovering the cookies before Marley.

Your boyfriend's inside the cottage. I can smell him.

I wasn't wrong about the howl. "Don't sound so disappointed."

I'm not a fan of the wolf form. Gives me the heebie jeebies.

"Help us break the spell, and you won't have to worry about it anymore."

Raoul cast a mournful look at the cottage. *I really wanted Pop-Tarts.*

"Then I guess you have to decide which is more important—your aversion to wolves or your fondness for tarts."

I think Wyatt Nash would have a tougher time answering that.

I opened the door and ushered my familiar inside. The cottage was dark and quiet. Marley must've gone to bed. I climbed the staircase to my bedroom where PP3 was curled up against the wolf. I stood in the doorway and smiled at the sight of the two cuddle buddies.

"Doesn't leave much room for me," I whispered.

The wolf scooted to the far side of the bed.

"Why Mr. Wolf, what big eyes you have," I said.

Granger closed his eyes.

Laughing, I went into the bathroom to change into pajamas, brush my teeth, and remove the debris from my hair. I peered at my reflection. There seemed to be a strand of white in my hair that I hadn't noticed before. Maybe it wasn't an effect of the spell. Maybe it was even worse—actual aging. I shuddered and turned away from the mirror.

By the time I climbed into bed, PP3 had migrated to the foot, leaving plenty of space for me to snuggle with the wolf. I buried my face in his thick coat, which seemed more unhygienic than it probably was.

"I'm going to find a way to get you back," I promised.

He responded by licking my cheek.

"You didn't lick your butt with that tongue, did you?"

He pushed me with a paw.

I laughed. "Just checking."

I fell asleep to the sound of his gentle panting, the rhythm matching the steady drumbeat of my heart.

Chapter Thirteen

Despite Granger's calming presence beside me, my dreams were filled with terrors. A bonfire in the woods interrupted by screams. Blood spatter. A body fighting against restraints. Ominous chanting.

I bolted upright and noticed that my hands were sticky with sweat. It seemed that Bertram Lapp's death had fused with the coven's failed spell and wormed their way into my subconscious in the form of nightmares. Terrific.

The wolf was gone by the time I awoke. He'd probably retreated into the woods before sunrise. I hated this for him.

Desperate times called for desperate measures. I cooked eggs and bacon for breakfast, which delighted Marley and PP3. Once Marley left for school, I made myself presentable. My hair seemed to be getting worse. I leaned forward to inspect my reflection. Yep. There definitely seemed to be more white strands in the cold light of day.

The mirror spell was stagnant, or so we believed. Maybe there was a slow progression that hadn't been perceptible. I'd have to ask Carly if her feet had grown even larger overnight.

I parked on the street parallel to Seers Row. I hadn't been to see the Voice of the Gods in quite some time. The shrieking seer was what my father would've called "a real character."

I passed another psychic storefront on my way to see Veronica. This one seemed to be taking advantage of the current situation because the sign in the window trumpeted a variety of reasons to schedule a reading, including the promise of an answer to—*find out how long the spell will last.*

I paused outside the door. What if it was more than a marketing ploy? What if this psychic knew something about the spell, or was even the cause of it? Some psychics also possessed magical abilities, although I highly doubted they were capable of the kind of magic that influenced everyone in town, unless they'd discovered an ancient artifact in their search for a new scrying glass.

Okay, my imagination was clearly working overtime this week. Still, I decided to pop inside and ask a couple questions. That was the reason I was here to speak to Veronica. Might as well make the most of it.

A bell jingled as I opened the door. If I'd visited this establishment before, I didn't remember it. The interior was relatively dark, and the primary color was pink in all shades, which seemed like a strange choice. The chairs were made of a plush magenta material. The tablecloth was bubblegum pink. Even the walls were painted the pale shade of a ballerina slipper.

"Can I help you?" a voice chirped. A petite blonde emerged from behind the counter. Her outfit was three shades of pink, including her knee-high boots. She looked close to my age, although with the spell it was hard to know for sure. She could be an eighty-year-old who still saw herself as she was in her youth.

"I saw your sign," I told her. "I'm wondering if you can tell me more about when the spell will end."

Her gaze raked over me. "Oh, I can see why you'd be anxious to know the answer to that. Have a seat."

I bristled. "What makes you think I want it to end? Maybe I want it to last indefinitely?"

"With that hair, I don't think so." She smiled despite the cutting words. "I'm Monica."

Monica and Veronica. Noted.

"I don't think we've met before," I said. "Have you set up shop recently?" A newcomer could be suspicious. All the more reason to ask a few questions.

"About two months ago. I moved from Petunia Lakes after my boyfriend cheated." She winced at the memory. "I wanted a fresh start."

"And you didn't see it coming?"

She rolled her eyes. "Why does everybody ask that? Of course not. We psychics never see our own fate. Do you know a healer that's successfully diagnosed themselves?"

Fair enough.

"Why do you have such a strong interest in ending the spell?" Monica asked. She reached for my hand. "May I?"

I let her examine my palm. "You don't want to use the crystal ball?"

"Please don't call it that. I can tell you know better."

I did, but I was testing her. I didn't know why I felt the need to poke her. I usually reserved such behavior for Aunt Hyacinth. Oh, who was I kidding? In New Jersey, if you're not born poking people, they run tests.

"I've heard of this, but I've never seen it before," Monica said, staring at my palm.

"It's a chicken pox scar."

"No, not that." She pointed to the lines on my hand. "You have sister lines. Two life lines."

I immediately thought of Claire in *Outlander*, which of course turned to thoughts of Jamie in a kilt.

"Tell me more," I urged. "Any chance I might time travel to Scotland?"

"I don't believe in time travel," she scoffed. "This indicates something else."

I didn't know how to read palms, but I took a stab at the meaning. "It's probably because I've lived in both the human world and the paranormal one. I grew up not knowing this world existed."

Monica chewed her lip. "Could be."

"That doesn't have anything to do with the mirror spell though. That happened way before."

Monica traced one of the lines with her fingernail, producing a shiver in me. "I think this does have to do with the spell. Can I see your other hand?"

I presented my other hand and watched her face as she compared them.

"Only one hand has the sister lines." She squeezed my right hand. "I think this one has the original lines." She squeezed my left hand. "This one has additional lines from the spell."

"What would that even mean?"

She stared at the left palm. "I have no idea."

I tugged my hand away. "Then I guess you can't tell me when the spell will end either."

Monica brightened. "Oh, sure I can. It'll break tomorrow before sundown."

I eyed her closely. "That's very specific. Do you know how?"

"No, only that it will break then."

"How do you know that?"

"Because I'm psychic. Duh."

"Yes, but did you see it in a vision? How did this information come to you?"

Monica leaned back to regard me. "Why does it matter? You asked when, and I told you."

"Because I'm investigating the source of the spell, so if there's a chance you know the identity of the caster, then I need that information."

Monica's face flickered with understanding. "I see. Well, I don't know the caster. I overheard another psychic tell someone when the spell would finally break. I've been using it to my advantage."

"Which psychic?"

She pointed to the wall. "Veronica, the Voice of the Gods."

It figured.

"Are you even a real psychic?" I demanded.

She nodded exuberantly. "Absolutely. I predicted my mom's third divorce, and the unfortunate death of my little brother's hamster. After that, I decided to get my certification online."

"You studied palmistry on a computer?"

"Sure. Why not? You can learn anything virtually nowadays."

I wasn't sure I agreed with that. "I don't think I'd want my surgeon to have learned online."

Monica rolled her eyes. "Your heart looks the same on a computer screen as it does in your chest. I bet you still write your schedule by hand too."

"Ha! Shows how much you know. I don't even keep a schedule."

Monica stared at me for a beat. "If you're interested in asking questions about the spell, I'd go see Veronica."

"That was my original plan. I got lured in by your sign."

She broke into a wide smile. "Oh, awesome. That means my marketing is working. It's called a hook."

"It's called fraud, but whatever."

I left Monica's pink palace and continued to Veronica's. The seer's ability to allegedly channel the voice of the gods was the only reason I continued to return to her. It certainly wasn't her sparkling personality.

The place was empty when I entered. There was no sign of Veronica or her intrepid assistant, Jericho. The interior was relatively sparse, with a round table covered in a purple cloth and two chairs. A new abstract painting hung on the wall. I wasn't generally a fan of that style of art, but the colors were pleasing to the eye.

"Hello?" I called.

A strapping man sauntered into the room from the back office. He reminded me of a prince from a fairy tale. His lush brown hair skimmed his shoulders, and his bone structure would've made Michelangelo weep. "Are you here for a reading?" his deep voice rumbled.

"Yes, is Veronica available?"

"One moment, please." He stuck his head into the back room. "Babe, you've got a customer."

"I'll be right there, sweetness," a voice sang to him.

I didn't blame her for sounding so joyful. This guy probably made her sing in more ways than one.

"What happened to Jericho?" No doubt he got fed up with being treated like gum on Veronica's spiked heel and finally left.

"I'm Jericho," the prince said.

I nearly tripped over my own feet. I didn't know why I

was so surprised. If Bolan viewed himself as buff and tall, why not Jericho?

Veronica emerged from the back room, her face aglow. The beautiful seer looked the same to me. Also not a surprise. She struck me as someone who had confidence in spades. She stood on her tiptoes and kissed Jericho's cheek as she passed him.

"You're here for a reading, I understand."

"I am." No matter how many times I came here, Veronica never seemed to remember me.

"Have a seat," she said, gesturing to the table. "Jericho, my love, will you be a darling and fetch my scrying glass?"

"Anything for you, dearest." Jericho ducked into the back room.

"Isn't he dashing?" Veronica fanned herself with her phone. "He's a dream come true. Whoever cast that spell deserves the key to the town."

He was still the same Jericho inside. "Not everyone is as happy about the spell."

She flicked a perfectly manicured fingernail painted black. "Oh, I know, but I'm happy, and so is he. In our little corner of the world, that's all that matters."

Jericho returned with the scrying glass in the palm of his hand. The Jericho I knew would have struggled to carry it at all. He set the orb on the stand on the table, then placed a hand on Veronica's arm. "Anything else, babe?"

She squeezed his hand. "Not right now, thank you."

There was no shrieking. No negative remarks. Jericho's new appearance had turned Veronica into a fawn. I wasn't sure what it said about Veronica that she was willing to treat this version of Jericho with such tenderness. It wasn't my relationship, though, and I had other matters to attend to.

"Is it true that the spell will end tomorrow before sundown?" I asked.

She arched a thin eyebrow. "Where did you hear that?"

"Word on the psychic street."

She inhaled through her nostrils. "I looked into the matter to see what I could learn, and that's what the gods told me."

"Do you believe it?"

She shifted in her chair. "I said it, didn't I?"

I wondered whether she was upset because, when the spell broke, Jericho would revert to his diminutive stature.

"I guess we can stop trying to break the spell if it's going to happen anyway," I said nonchalantly.

"Good idea. Stop trying. It's futile."

"Babe," Jericho's voice floated out from the back room.

Veronica's eyes flashed with irritation. "Did I forget to mention the second part?"

"There's a second part?"

"If the spell isn't broken by sundown, then the magic will be permanent." She leaned back and smiled in Jericho's general direction. "Happy now?"

"Honesty is the best policy," he sang back.

I was stuck on the second part. "The gods told you that?"

"That's why they call me the Voice of the Gods."

No wonder she didn't want to tell me. Veronica basically admitted she had no reason to want the spell broken.

"Do you know anything about palmistry and two life lines?" I asked.

She pulled a face. "Are you here for the Voice of the Gods, or are you here for a carnival con artist?"

"Voice of the Gods," I mumbled.

"Good." Veronica nodded toward the orb. "Please place both hands on the glass. Fuel the orb with your energy."

I followed her instructions and was taken aback when she covered my hands with her own. Her technique had changed.

She closed her eyes and slowed her breathing. She seemed to fall into some sort of trance.

"So much power," she murmured.

That was Ivy's magic she felt, not mine. Well, arguably it was mine now, but it didn't feel that way. I still associated it with my ancient ancestor.

Veronica's eyes flew open. "No!" she yelled and pushed the scrying glass off the table. I jumped from my chair to avoid it landing on my foot. The orb dropped to the floor with a heavy thud and rolled away.

Jericho rushed to her side. "Turtle dove? What's the matter?"

Veronica's breathing was labored now, and her gaze was pinned to me. "You must stop," she told me.

"Stop what?" I picked up the scrying glass and returned it the table.

"No more magic," she warned. "Too dangerous."

"I'm not here to do magic."

The color drained from Veronica's face. "Your magic will wreak havoc."

Jericho ruffled her hair. "You're such a poet, my love."

Veronica ignored her lover's attention, maintaining eye contact with me. "You must listen. Magic is a weight that will bury you."

My blood turned cold. That happened to Ivy, not me. It was possible Veronica was reading the past and not the future. Or maybe Ivy's magic included some of her memories. There was so much we still didn't know about magic. Some declared death was life's greatest mystery, but Aunt Hyacinth said on more than one occasion that she believed it was magic.

The seer backed away slowly. "You should leave now. I have another appointment, and I need to prepare."

"I haven't paid."

"No charge." She bolted from the room like I might electrocute her if she stayed.

Jericho looked at me, his eyes brimming with curiosity. "What was that about?"

"I don't know. I came to ask about the mirror spell. I'm working with the sheriff's office to find the caster so we can undo it." Or I could wait and see if the spell broke on its own like the seer said. That didn't seem likely though.

Jericho's face fell. "I was worried about that."

"I can see why. You seem content with the situation."

"Can you blame me?" He glanced at the empty doorway through which Veronica had retreated. "I've been in love with her since the moment I met her. When the opportunity arose that allowed her to see me as I see myself, naturally, I seized it with both strong hands." He made two fists.

Strong, indeed. It was hard not to let my imagination wander when looking at his hands, wondering what they were capable of. I shook off the inappropriate line of thought and prayed Granger returned to his human form soon.

"What will happen when the spell breaks?" I asked.

Jericho offered a rueful smile. "I have no illusions about that. I'll go back to looking the way the world sees me."

"Yes, but the question is—will it still be the way

Veronica sees you?" Could the spell permanently change her view of her devoted assistant?

"I'm not thinking of the future," he said firmly. "I'm living in the present moment, and enjoying every second of it while it lasts, even if it's only one more day. Nothing is permanent anyway."

"Maybe not, but is it real?"

"It's real while it lasts, no? When she whispers in my ear and calls me darling, she means it." A pleasant smile passed his lips. "And no matter what happens next, I'll have the memories to keep me warm at night."

I stared at him, trying to keep any sympathy from my expression. I wasn't sure how he'd maintain that healthy attitude once she was well and truly gone—at least in a romantic sense. He'd be forced to watch her move on to someone else. Why invite that kind of pain?

"You're hoping she isn't as superficial as she seems," I said.

His broad shoulders sagged ever so slightly. "What's that old proverb? If not for hope, the heart would break."

I felt a rush of sadness for him. "Good luck, Jericho. I hope things work out for you."

"I'd say the same to you, but I'd prefer you take as long as possible to undo the spell." His mouth turned up at the corners. "For obvious reasons."

"Just remember, you're still this prince ... I mean, this paranormal on the inside, and that's the part of you she's fallen in love with. All the new package has done is given her a chance to finally see you as you really are."

"You're very kind, Ms. Rose."

"You remember me?"

"Of course. I remember everyone who walks through

that door. One of my many gifts." He looked forlornly at the empty doorway.

"Jericho, my sweet," Veronica's voice rang out. "Come here, please. I miss you."

"I miss you too, my love," he said softly, and went to join her.

Chapter Fourteen

My phone rang as I climbed behind the steering wheel of my car. Bolan's name appeared on the screen. I turned on the car and switched to speaker mode.

"Hey, Deputy. What's up?"

"I'm stuck at a dental appointment, but I learned from Jeremiah that there was a name missing from my list. Howard Lapp."

"Brother?"

"Cousin. He was at the party, but he left early, before the spell hit. Turns out he and the victim co-owned a family orchard together."

Not anymore.

"Based on the records I saw," Bolan continued, "ownership of the orchard isn't a hugely profitable venture, unless one of them discovered secret treasure on the property."

"At this point, I wouldn't rule it out. You want me to talk to him?"

"If you don't mind. Might not be a coincidence that he left early. My mouth is going to be numb for hours."

"You sound fine to me, just a little dopey, but that's probably the drugs."

"I'm still in the waiting room, Rose. I haven't had my turn yet."

Oops. "Okay, send me the address, and I'll check him out."

I turned on Thistle Road and drove to a compact neighborhood to the west of downtown. Howard Lapp's house was charming. The stone facade and brick chimney reminded me of homes in the English countryside. The front door was painted black and so glossy that I was afraid to touch it in case it was wet. I rang the bell instead.

The door split open a minute later, and I heard a voice call, "In here."

The interior was snug, so it wasn't hard to locate the source. I entered the cramped room that seemed to serve as both a small library and an office.

Howard Lapp sat in a chair by the desk, his weight spilling over the edges. His wings were the color of a faded bruise and looked too small for his body. He adjusted his posture, clearly uncomfortable, whether from the chair or the unexpected company, I wasn't sure.

"Good morning, Mr. Lapp," I said, adopting a tone that was polite yet firm. It was the voice I'd been practicing on strangers ever since Marley accused me of being "too aggressive" with cashiers and service providers.

"Good morning," he replied, although he didn't look too sure about it.

"My name is Ember Rose. I'm here on behalf of the sheriff's office to ask you a few questions about your cousin's death." I set my business card on the desk.

He didn't bother to look at it. "What do you want to

know?" His voice trembled slightly. Maybe Howard was hiding something after all.

I settled into the chair opposite him. "You were at the restaurant for Bertram's party." I left the statement dangling between us.

"Of course. It was his birthday, and I'm his cousin."

"Were you two close?"

Howard scowled. "Not as close as he and Eugene, but close enough. We celebrated holidays together and sometimes took vacations."

I sensed friction between Howard and Bert's best friend. Interesting.

"I understand you left the restaurant before the spell hit."

"A good thing, too."

"Why's that?" I asked.

He closed his eyes and scrunched his face in a ball of embarrassment. "Isn't it obvious?"

"I haven't met you before, Mr. Lapp. I don't know how you'd normally look."

"Well, I'm about a hundred pounds heavier than I was last week, according to the scale."

Ah. "I guess you've been seeing yourself as overweight."

Howard's face reddened. "Every time I looked in the mirror, I saw an old, fat fairy. I stopped letting anybody take photos of me because I couldn't stand seeing them on social media later. I felt embarrassed."

I couldn't help but sympathize with him. "And the spell made you look the way you saw yourself."

"That's my understanding. They're calling it a reflection spell."

"Or mirror spell," I mumbled. "Some paranormals are calling it that."

"Whatever they call it, I hope it's over soon. I promise that I'll never call myself fat again." He wobbled the extra flab of his stomach. "And to think I thought I was fat before."

"I'm sure you're not the only one making promises to themselves."

His gaze flicked to me. "I guess you're worried about aging prematurely."

My fingers stroked strands of my hair. "Why would you say that?"

He quickly seemed to realize his error. "Oh, I thought the spell … never mind."

I straightened in my seat. "Why don't we talk about the reason for my visit—the death of your cousin?"

Howard's wings fluttered at the mention of the victim. "What's this about anyway? Why is the sheriff sending someone to ask me questions?"

His question took me off guard. "Wouldn't you like to know who killed your cousin?"

"Who killed him? Bert died of natural causes."

I frowned. "What makes you say that?"

Howard suddenly grew flustered. "How could it be anything else?"

"Haven't you spoken to anyone since he died?"

"No, I've been hiding here until the spell breaks. I don't want anyone to see me."

"You haven't talked on the phone or texted anyone?"

"Jeremiah called the next day to tell me he died. He didn't say what happened."

"And you didn't ask?"

"I didn't want to upset him any more than he already was. I figured the reason didn't matter."

Or you already knew the reason.

"I figured the boys would call me when they were ready to plan the service." He paused. "And Eugene, too, I guess." I didn't miss the trace of bitterness in his voice when he mentioned the best friend.

"Why did you leave early?"

Howard fidgeted. "I wasn't in the mood to stay."

"You realize it looks suspicious, don't you?"

Howard blinked rapidly. "You think I killed my cousin? How? I wasn't there. I don't even know how he died."

"You left the scene of the crime before the spell hit and before Bertram died. Doesn't that seem convenient?"

"If I left before he died, how did I kill him?"

"You tell me. How did you manage to choke him without anybody seeing you? An invisibility cloak?"

Howard looked stricken. "Bert was strangled? That's so awful." He seemed to come to his senses. "I left early because I was seated at the opposite end of the table from where I wanted to be."

"So you took your ball and went home?"

"More or less. Bert was between Eugene and Jeremiah. I was stuck at the other end with the kid from Bert's office. Nice guy but not the reason I was there."

"It seems like Bertram and Eugene were friends for a long time," I said carefully.

Howard scowled. "Bert and I were best friends when we were kids. Our dads were twins and spent a lot of time together, so it was bound to happen."

I thought of my relationships with Florian, Aster, and Linnea. They'd been indispensable to me since the day I met them. "Sounds like you were very fond of your cousin."

Howard wiped a stray tear from his eye. "I miss him so much already. I still feel like he's going to show up at my house for a round of late-night poker." He chuckled.

"Well, late night for us is more like five o'clock these days."

"I feel you," I said. There were days that my pajamas beckoned to me at six o'clock. "When Eugene entered the picture, that must've changed your friendship with Bertram."

Howard nodded. "It was the three of us for years, but slowly, they started to ice me out. I know it was Eugene though. Bert loved me like a brother. He never would've decided to do that on his own. He was too kindhearted."

It struck me that Bertram would've made more of an effort to keep Howard in the mix if he truly felt that way, but there was nothing to gain by giving voice to my thoughts, so I stayed silent.

"Do you have any reason to think Eugene might've harmed your cousin?" It was worth hearing Howard's point of view, however tainted. Sometimes it revealed more about the speaker than the subject.

Howard took a long time before answering. Finally, he said, "As much as I'd love to point the finger at him, the only reason I can think of is Carly, but Eugene wasn't so desperate that he'd kill his best friend over it. The three of them seemed to settle into some weird love triangle without the angst."

"I met Carly. I have to admit, I can understand why they didn't want to rock the boat."

"Beautiful inside and out, I agree." Howard wiped the sweat from his brow with the back of his hand. "I can't believe somebody would do that to Bert. What did the boys have to say about it? I assume you spoke to them already."

"We have." I didn't feel the need to disclose what we learned. "I understand you owned property jointly with your cousin, isn't that right?"

"Yes, the Happy Orchard. We inherited it from our dads. What about it?" His brow furrowed. "Do you think I killed Bert to take control of the orchard?" He belly laughed, resting his hands on the swell of his stomach.

"Murders have been committed for less," I pointed out.

"I know, but it's not like it makes a profit. It's more to do with sentimental value."

"Just because it isn't profitable doesn't mean the land itself isn't valuable. If you sold it, you could make a mint."

"I guess that's true, except I don't get the whole property anyway. Bert's half will be divided between his sons, and I'll maintain my half. That's the way the agreement was written."

He was right. There was no incentive for Howard to kill his cousin for the orchard. "Can you think of any reason someone might want to hurt your cousin?"

The large fairy sighed. "I would know if there was, but no one comes to mind. What did Eugene say?"

"His suggestion was a dead end." I hesitated. "It's none of my business, but you might want to consider reaching out to Eugene. You both lost someone special to you. Maybe you can reminisce together." I would've liked to have someone to commiserate with after my father died. Karl too. I was alone, though, and they'd been challenging times for me. Sometimes I looked back and was amazed that I'd made it through at all.

"You're right. I should invite him to play cards. I'm sure he's missing Bert as much as I am." The button in the middle of his shirt popped open, exposing Howard's bare skin. Groaning, he tried to close the fabric without success. "But I think I'll wait until this spell is reversed and we can all go back to normal." He eyed me closely. "Any idea when that might happen?"

"We're working on it," I said truthfully. I omitted Veronica's premonition since I had no idea how accurate it was.

Howard struggled to his feet, nearly pitching forward from the weight of his stomach. "From where I'm sitting, it can't happen soon enough."

My stomach grumbled as I left Howard's house, and I decided to return downtown to grab a sandwich from the deli near my old office. The deli's famous chicken salad on a croissant was one of the many things I missed about working as a reporter for *Vox Populi*.

"Hey, it's Ember Rose," the deli owner declared when I entered. "We thought you'd given us up for good."

"You can't get rid of me that easily, Joel."

Truth be told, I avoided the deli for fear of crossing paths with Alec, but like the broomstick, I knew it was time to reclaim my joy—and if that included chicken salad on a croissant, then so be it.

"What do you think about this spell?" Joel asked as he prepared my sandwich. "Crazy, huh?"

"How were you affected?" I couldn't tell from this side of the counter.

Joel craned his neck to give me a knowing smile. "Let's just say, my romantic life has improved dramatically this week."

I peered over the counter for a better view. He looked the same from the back. It was only when he pivoted to face me that I understood.

"Oh, wow," I said.

He grinned. "That's what she said. I even had to buy new boxer briefs. They needed stretchier fabric."

My eyes snapped back to his face. It seemed rude to

stare at the massive bulge. "Well, it was nice to see you again, Joel." I kept my gaze firmly at eye level as he handed me the bag containing my sandwich. I refused to glance down at my purse to find the right amount of money. I didn't want to risk another glimpse of the trouser python. I tossed money on the counter and hoped for the best.

"Come back soon," Joel called after me.

I couldn't escape fast enough. I pushed open the door and tore around the corner, arriving in the alleyway that ran behind the strip of buildings that housed *Vox Populi*.

Two red eyes glowed in the shadows. My breath caught in my throat. I fumbled for my wand, before realizing I didn't have it. Never mind. My magic was powerful enough on its own. I only liked the wand to help me focus and not create a magical catastrophe—like the one who cast the mirror spell.

"Back away," I said in a firm voice. "You wouldn't like me when I go full Jersey."

The eyes remained exactly in the same spot. I heard a guttural sound that made the hairs on the back of my neck stand on end. I clutched the bag with my sandwich because no way was I willing to lose it.

"I'm warning you. I have magic, and I'm not afraid to use it."

The figure cut through the shadows. The creature's fangs were longer and sharper than a normal vampire's. His face was paler, and his cheekbones were more pronounced. If it weren't for the custom suit that I'd seen him wear a dozen times, I might not have recognized him.

"Alec?" I said softly.

This distorted version of a vampire was my former boss and boyfriend, Alec Hale. No surprise this was how the mirror spell impacted him. He'd always believed himself to be more monstrous than he truly was.

The monster version of Alec snarled at me. I didn't react. If I stayed calm, he wouldn't pounce. That was my theory, anyway.

"Alec, it's me, Ember."

Another snarl.

"Have you been wandering around in this state ever since the spell hit?"

As he loomed over me, I caught a whiff of his pungent scent. There were stains on his suit. I had the sinking feeling he'd been wearing the same clothes for days.

"Has anybody been helping you?" I thought of Granger, wandering around town in his wolf form. At least he had me to tend to him. Alec seemed to be completely on his own.

You reap what you sow, I thought and immediately felt guilty for my lack of compassion.

Alec continued to tower over me without saying or doing anything. Despite his intimidating presence, he didn't seem to want to hurt me.

"Listen," I said. "I know you, probably better than anybody. Just because you think you're a monster on the inside doesn't mean you have to act like one. The spell reflects the way we see ourselves, but our actions are what define us, not how we look. You can have enormous fangs and still not use them to hurt someone."

The tension seemed to ease from the creature's broad shoulders.

"You're not going to bite me, Alec." My tone was firm and no nonsense. It occurred to me that he must be hungry. With a pang of regret, I opened my bag. "Croissandwich?" I held it up for his inspection.

Alec sniffed the contents of the bag.

"It isn't blood, but there are red grapes in the chicken salad." It was the best I could do. I wasn't about to slice open a vein.

Alec swiped the bag from my grasp and tore into the croissant with a ravenous hunger.

"You're murdering that poor chicken all over again," I said.

The sandwich disappeared in under twenty seconds. I'd been right about the hunger. The red in his eyes seemed to fade to a lighter pink.

"Can you speak?" I asked. With those ridiculous fangs, it was hard to tell.

He opened his mouth. "I ... I haven't tried."

It was Alec's voice, only slightly raspier. "There you are," I told him. "It's okay, Alec. *You're* okay."

His brow creased. "I'm sorry if I frightened you. That wasn't my intention." His voice was barely above a whisper.

"I know. It took me a hot second, but I figured out it was you."

"I didn't know where to go. I feel like I've been having an out-of-body experience."

"I can only imagine. Did you go to the office?"

He nodded. "Bentley and Fiona called the police when I walked through the door. I was so startled by their reaction that I took off."

"How did they look?"

"Bentley's ears were pointier, and he was taller. Fiona was younger, and her wings brighter." The more he spoke, the more normal he sounded.

I smiled at his descriptions. "That tracks." I missed my former colleagues. Despite my sibling-style rivalry with the elf, I genuinely liked Bentley.

He touched my hair. "You've gone blond. Trying to blend in with the rest of your family?"

"The alley light is being kind to me. It's a few strands of white."

His brow furrowed. "From where I'm standing, it matches the color of Hyacinth's hair."

I laughed. "I don't think so."

"Use your phone."

I pulled out my phone and held up the screen in camera mode. I gasped at the sight of my head. There was now an entire layer of white-blond hair that covered my head like a snow-capped mountain.

"How?" I asked. "I don't know what's happening. I didn't do this."

"If it's any consolation, it suits you, or it will when it all grows in."

"Thank you, but I'd much rather keep my natural hair." Whatever this was, it couldn't be good. "Did your condition worsen over time?"

"If anything, it's gotten better. I just needed someone else to see me the way they do." A smile touched his lips. "I'm glad it was you."

"I'm just glad someone snapped you out of it. You reek. Go home and shower before you're arrested as a public health threat."

He gazed at me with as much tenderness as his monstrous face allowed. "You should visit us for lunch one day. I'm sure Tanya and Bentley would be thrilled to spend time with you."

I angled my head at him. "Tanya and Bentley, huh?" Typical Alec. He'd tell me others missed me but never him. That would make him too vulnerable. The vampire shied away from anything that made him feel... Well, I'd stop right there. Anything that made him 'feel' made him uncomfortable. My relationship with Granger was so much easier by comparison. I didn't have to beg the werewolf to fully participate in the relationship. He showed up for me every day, effortlessly. A part of me would always love Alec, but it was the kind of love that was a noun rather than a verb.

"Take care of yourself, Ember. Stay safe."

"You too." I retreated from the alleyway, once again aware of my own hunger. There was no way I was willing to return to the deli and face the trouser python. I cut my losses and headed for home.

Chapter Fifteen

I returned to Rose Cottage feeling a mixture of discomfort and defeat. My run-in with Alec had unsettled me. At least I ruled out another suspect. There was no way Howard Lapp could've moved fast enough to strangle Bertram and leave the restaurant undetected. A minor win.

Rose Cottage was quiet when I entered. I had no doubt Marley was sequestered in her bedroom with headphones on, doing her homework. I whistled for PP3, but the Yorkie remained on the sofa, only bothering to open one eye.

"Marley already took you out, I guess."

The dog closed his eye and returned to his catatonic state.

The kitchen door swung open, and Raoul waddled into the living room carrying an oversized drumstick.

"Are you time traveling?" I asked. "It looks like you stole food from the king's banquet hall."

With his sharp teeth, he tore meat from the bone and chewed. *There's an amazing restaurant called Feast that only serves medieval food. Their dumpster is my new favorite place.*

"Maybe you should take Granger. He might appreciate a turkey leg in his current state."

Raoul leveled me with a look. *Would you honestly be able to kiss a mouth that made contact with a medieval dumpster?*

"Good point. On second thought, let's not tell him about it."

Raoul made short work of the large drumstick and licked the bone. *What's up with your hair? You look like a snow cone.*

"Gee, thanks."

How's the investigation?

"You mean the investigation you're supposed to be helping with? You're the second R in R&R, or have you forgotten?"

I'm with you in spirit. The raccoon set the bone on top of a coaster on the coffee table. *Here's a crazy idea. Why don't we try to summon the dead guy's spirit?*

I stared at him. "Where'd you get that idea?"

I may have landed on your altar when I climbed down from the window and knocked one of your books to the floor, and that book may have opened to a page with a summoning spell.

I folded my arms. "Do you think by trying to turn an accident into a sign from the gods that I won't be annoyed?"

That depends. Did it work?

"If it were that simple, we'd summon a spirit every time somebody was murdered and ask for details."

Maybe the sheriff should rethink his investigative strategies or be replaced by a magic user.

"I'm sure he'd love to hear your suggestion."

Raoul's eyes widened. *He isn't here, is he? I didn't smell him when I came in.*

"I don't think so." I pondered his idea. "Seriously, what makes you think a summoning spell would do the trick?"

Because this murder is different.

I shot him a quizzical look. "Different how?"

Raoul settled on the sofa cushion next to PP3. The dog sniffed the air and started to lick Raoul's paw. *If his death was connected to the spell or the result of supernatural causes, that would make it more likely his ghost is lurking around town.*

I debated the possibility. At this point, I was willing to try anything within reason. "Why not? I don't have anything better to do." Certainly not while Granger was trapped in wolf form. My evenings were going to be far less enjoyable for the foreseeable future.

Raoul sank against a pillow. *You know where we keep the candles. You'll need seven.*

"You're not even going to help me gather the materials?"

You saw the size of that turkey drumstick. I need a power nap before we attempt to summon a spirit.

Shaking my head, I went to find the necessary items. The candles were in the kitchen cabinet. I found Ivy's grimoire still open on the floor.

You couldn't be bothered to pick up the book? I asked.

Trying to nap here, remember?

Why do you think I'm using telepathy? That's my literal inside voice.

The raccoon sighed. *I didn't want to risk losing the page, so I did you a favor and left it open. How confident would you be if you had to recite the spell from memory?*

I couldn't even do the multiplication table from memory

in third grade. I swiped the book from the floor and tucked it under my arm.

Good luck reading Ivy's medieval script, Raoul said, yawning. *The only reason I knew it was seven candles is because of the picture.*

I smiled. He wasn't wrong about the handwriting. The contents of Ivy's books had originally been concealed by magic, so we were fortunate to be able to read anything at all.

I made sure to grab a bite to eat before I started to feel sick to my stomach. Nothing looked as appetizing as the turkey leg, but then I was reminded it came from a dumpster, and suddenly the leftover egg salad in my fridge looked more appealing.

By the time I placed everything we needed in a neat pile on the coffee table, Raoul was in the process of waking up. He stretched his furry arms over his head and yawned again. *Good job*, he said. *You should probably get a backpack to make everything easier to carry.*

"Carry where?"

The woods.

"What's wrong with the cottage?"

Where do I start? That rug is hideous. He paused. *Oh, you mean for the summoning. The closer to nature the better, don't you think?*

"I guess you're right." I removed a cardigan from the back of a dining chair and slid my arms through the sleeves.

Marley thundered down the steps, prompting PP3 to lift his weary head. She wore large headphones around the back of her neck.

"Why the stampede?" I asked.

"I finished my homework."

"And what—you're throwing yourself a parade?"

She ignored my remark. "Can I go to Caffeinated Cauldron? Some friends from school are meeting there in half an hour."

"Do you have a ride?"

"Yes." Marley suddenly noticed the collection of candles and other items on the coffee table. "What's going on?"

"Raoul and I have decided to channel the spirit of Bertram Lapp and ask his ghost what happened to him."

She snorted. "Like that would work."

Raoul and I shrugged in unison.

Marley gaped at me. "You're serious? How is that an option?"

"Why not? It happened during a supernatural event. There's a chance the death was connected to the spell, which increases the chances of his spirit sticking around."

Marley seemed to consider my argument. "I thought the cause of death was choking."

"Strangulation."

"He was in the middle of dinner," Marley said matter-of-factly. "Maybe the examiner was wrong."

"His neck was bruised," I told her. "Last I checked your food doesn't fight back."

Speak for yourself, Raoul said.

Marley's face reflected her inner conflict. Finally, she said, "That actually sounds more fun than the coffee shop. Can I help?"

No, Raoul said. *We're all stocked up on Roses.*

"Absolutely," I told her. Although we didn't need her for the spell, I liked the idea of mother-daughter bonding via spirit summoning. It seemed like a very Starry Hollow thing to do. Aunt Hyacinth would be proud.

Marley's phone lit up in her hand, and she gazed at the screen in consternation. "No fair," she whined.

"What is it?"

She chewed her bottom lip. "I think I'll go to the coffee shop after all."

I started to suspect a romantic reason for her interest in tonight's social gathering. "Up to you," I said casually.

The heart wants what the heart wants, Raoul said, not sounding the least bit bothered by her change in plans.

"I'm going to get changed," Marley announced, and bolted from the room.

Raoul clucked his tongue. *Dumping her mother for a boy. That can't feel good.*

It feels like normal childhood development, I shot back. It was a relief, in fact. There'd been times when I worried that I'd live with Marley for the rest of my life, not that I didn't love her to pieces. I only wanted her to develop independence and her own life apart from me.

"Take Bonkers with you," I called after her. I'd feel better if she had her familiar with her.

"Okay," came the faint reply.

I pivoted to Raoul with my hands on my hips. "What's your problem? Why are you being so territorial tonight?"

He started to sulk. *Because three's a crowd.*

A low growl escaped from PP3.

"You're not the only one who feels that way, apparently."

Raoul climbed down from the sofa. *Let's get this party started. Just you and me.*

PP3 remained perfectly still.

We walked through the woods behind the cottage until we found a suitable spot for the summoning spell. As I placed the white candles in a circle, I decided to dig a little deeper into Raoul's earlier comment. "What's really going on with you? Since when do you care if Marley joins us?"

Raoul scattered plants in the center of the circle. *You haven't had as much time for me lately. With the sheriff playing the Big Bad Wolf, I figured you and me would have the chance to spend more quality time together.*

"If that's how you feel, then why not take a greater role in the investigation?"

Because that's work. That's not quality time. We haven't gotten pizza or tacos together in ages, not without the werewolf. Don't get me wrong, I'm happy you two are together. He dropped to the ground on his bottom. *I'd just like to do more witch-familiar bonding, without stragglers.*

A lump formed in my throat. "I'm so sorry, Raoul. I never meant to make you feel like a third wheel. I'm glad you spoke up. I'll definitely make an effort to spend one-on-one time with you outside of a work setting."

It's no big deal, he mumbled. *I have other friends at the dump and all.*

"It is a big deal," I insisted, "and you're right. I shouldn't be ditching everyone else in favor of Granger. Relationships need to be balanced and fair to both parties. I didn't realize I was leaning so heavily in one direction."

Raoul's eyes glimmered in the darkness. *I'm probably feeling it more because ... I don't know. I guess because I don't have a sheriff, or a Marley, or a hellbeast.*

"You mean a dog?"

You say potato. I say hellbeast.

I smiled at him. "Raoul, you're my familiar. Do you know what that means?"

That I'm privy to raunchier thoughts than I'm comfortable with?

"Maybe that," I acknowledged, "but it also means you're

irreplaceable. Nobody else in this entire world can be my familiar. Only you." I leaned down and poked his stomach like he was the Pillsbury Doughboy.

When do you think you'll move in together?

"One issue at a time," I said. "There's no point in worrying about living arrangements while he's still peeing on fire hydrants." Okay, that was probably an exaggeration. Granger was a very well-behaved wolf.

I sat cross-legged on the ground outside the circle and groaned at the sound of a cracking knee.

You're too young for creaky joints, Raoul said.

"That's the nicest thing you've ever said to me."

He waved a paw at the candles. *Shouldn't you be inside the circle?*

"Not for this. The circle is to contain Bertram's spirit, assuming we can even summon him."

Raoul observed me from the side. *You're really hunched over when you sit with your legs crossed. Can't you sit up straighter?*

I glared at him. "When did you become Aunt Hyacinth?" I made an effort to straighten my back, but my body refused to comply.

You need to stretch more. You should try yoga. Or maybe meditation.

"I'm from New Jersey. We don't do that." I concentrated on the task at hand.

What can I do?

"I can't see the book in the dark, and I forgot my phone. Feed me my lines."

Now I'm hungry.

He opened the book to the marked page and began to read. I repeated each line and focused my magic on the circle. The wind blew through the trees and nearly extinguished the flames.

I hope this ghost shows up before we start a forest fire, Raoul said.

Magic thrashed inside me. It felt as though more magic was attempting to force its way out than what I'd channeled. I shifted on the ground. It was tricky to both push and pull magic at the same time.

Raoul watched me closely. *Is there a problem?*

I decided to release a small amount of magic and then stop. There was too much magic pressing against me.

The flames managed to blow out even from the small amount of magic I released, plunging us into complete darkness. I let go of my hold on the magic and felt it plummet inside me.

What are we waiting for?

"I wanted to see if that was enough magic to summon Bertram." Apparently not. "Ivy's magic is too strong. It's like I only want to turn the faucet far enough for a trickle, but something's pushing my hand to turn it all the way on."

Maybe you should give the magic what it wants.

"What's that supposed to mean? Summon every spirit in Starry Hollow?"

Raoul shrugged. *If that's what gets us the dead fairy.*

"We're going to need a bigger circle," I joked. There was no way I'd really broaden the spell and risk dragging dozens of spirits into the woods behind my house. That was a horror movie waiting to happen.

I dusted off my pants and rose to my feet.

What are you doing?

"I'm channeling my inner Kenny Rogers."

Raoul blinked his beady eyes.

I patted his head. "Knowing when to fold 'em. You

clearly didn't grow up with my father." He played *The Gambler* on repeat when I was a kid.

Giving up isn't very Rose-like, Raoul said. *I promise not to tell your aunt if you buy me pepperoni pizza, or tacos. I'm willing to negotiate.*

I bent over to collect the materials. "I think you're right about conjuring a spell that requires more juice. I just think it should be one with less risk of haunting the entire forest."

The book slipped from his paws and fell open. He crouched down to pick it up and stopped dead.

"What is it? Is there a spider on the page?" Raoul wasn't a big fan of our eight-legged friends.

What about talking to the actual dead guy? That would require way more magic than a summoning spell, right?

I cast a sidelong glance at the raccoon. "Are you suggesting what I think you're suggesting?"

He held up the book and tapped the page. *Necromancy requires powerful magic, or so I've heard.*

I hugged myself as another cool breeze blew past us. "You want me to try to raise the dead? That sounds riskier than summoning spirits."

Not if it's contained. He's not in the graveyard yet. This is Starry Hollow. How many bodies can the morgue have?

He made a good point.

Might help relieve the pressure of all that magic and help you catch the killer. Seems like a win-win to me.

I pondered the suggestion. "I'm pretty sure necromancy is one of those no-no's."

And you're such a rule follower? Since when?

I stuffed all the items into the backpack and slung it over my shoulder. "I'll think about it."

You can't take too long. The body isn't going to stay in

the morgue forever. For all we know, it could be gone tomorrow.

Another good point. "I'll find out."

As we walked home through the darkness, I was acutely aware of the power stirring within me. I thought I'd accepted Ivy's magic, yet there seemed to be a part of me that was resistant to its presence. Like white blood cells attacking a virus.

"You know what's weird?"

Aside from your hair?

I ignored him. "I thought I saw a spirit in the woods the other night when I was flying through the trees. I would've thought I'd at least have summoned that one to the circle with the amount of magic I released."

Are you sure it was a ghost?

"No. It could've been a shadow." And they'd seemed familiar, although it was hard to tell in the gloaming.

By the time we returned to the cottage, I'd made a decision. Between Alec, the summoning spell, and the memory of the shadowy figure, necromancy would be the cherry on a weird day sundae.

"Let's do it," I said to the raccoon.

You're sure?

"I'm sure. I mean, it's you and me doing it. What could go wrong?"

Chapter Sixteen

Outside the healer's office, I itched with anticipation. I was eager to test Raoul's theory about casting a spell that required more firepower. Then I'd see whether Ivy's magic calmed down. I disliked being so aware of it now. Magic shouldn't feel like a passenger, because then it was only a matter of time before it wanted to drive.

You're sure his body's still in there? Raoul asked.

"According to Bolan."

You asked him directly?

"I texted him to ask whether Howard Lapp could see his cousin in the morgue tomorrow. Bolan said if he showed up before ten a.m."

Raoul gave me a sidelong glance. *Why, Ember Rose, you sneaky devil.*

"How do you think I was able to sneak around with Karl behind my dad's back?"

Do you ever worry whether Marley will do the same to you?

I froze. "Please don't ever say those words to me again. That's nightmare material."

Normal child development, remember?

"The only child development that resulted from my behavior was the one that grew in my uterus."

Raoul cringed. *Please don't ever say those words to me again.*

My phone rang. I glanced at the screen to see Aster's name. I quickly rejected the call.

You don't want to tell her what we're doing? Maybe she'd want to help.

"Do you seriously think Aster would support this idea?" My cousin was the ultimate rule follower. She'd break out in hives at the mere thought of waking the dead. To be fair, I was surprised that I'd agreed to try. I wasn't rigid about rules, but I knew necromancy was frowned upon, yet here I was, ready and willing. Maybe I was evolving in the wrong direction. Nothing would surprise me when it came to—me.

Entering the building was simple with a basic unlocking spell. Security wasn't particularly tight in Starry Hollow, and the healer's office was no exception.

"I don't think this counts as breaking and entering because we're not breaking anything." I knew my flawed logic was a meager attempt to assuage the guilt I felt. Granger would be so disappointed in me. On the other hand, if we learned the truth straight from the corpse's mouth and cracked the case, everybody would be too relieved to ask follow-up questions.

Raoul stood on his hind legs and tried to read the plaques on the doors. *Where's the morgue?*

"Basement."

He shuddered. *Why do they have to put the dead bodies*

in the basement? It's bad enough they have to spend the rest of their existence underground.

I located the basement door, which was unlocked. I turned on the flashlight that I'd carried in the side pocket of my backpack.

Why not just flip the switch? You're not going to wake up anybody down there with a bright light. Raoul paused. *Although that would make our job much easier.*

I crept down the steps, listening intently for any sounds. It was as quiet as you'd expect.

I arrived at the bottom of the steps and swept the room with the beam of light.

The morgue isn't that creepy.

"It isn't exactly festive either." A chill tingled my spine. I wasn't sure what possessed me to think this was a good idea. Despite my misgivings, I set up camp while Raoul scampered through the room in search of Bertram's final resting slab.

My skin pricked as I emptied the contents of my backpack on the floor of the sterile room. Guilt continued to plague me, but I brushed it aside. There was no chance anyone would've let me try this experiment if I'd suggested it. I knew that fact was a red flag waving at me, yet I ignored it. I gently reminded myself that this was an opportunity to crack the case, as well as relieve the growing pressure of Ivy's magic. A win-win, as long as nothing went wrong.

No pressure.

You brought the book, right? Raoul asked.

I tugged Ivy's grimoire from the backpack. Ivy's spells were far more advanced than anything in my own books. With her magic in my possession, though, I figured I'd have the necessary skills to perform the spell.

"Did you find the body?" I asked.

Raoul tapped a locker. *Our friend's in here.*

"Are you sure?" The last thing we needed was to rouse the wrong corpse.

You're not the only one who can read. His name is right here. Raoul squinted at the label. *Oops. Hang on. Not this one.* He scooted to the next locker. *Next one.*

I groaned. "I'm ready."

Raoul pulled the handle and a slab slid out. Bertram Lapp stared at the ceiling. To my horror, the raccoon pulled himself onto the slab and climbed across the body.

"Raoul," I hissed. "What are you doing?"

I'm going to tie his shoelaces just in case.

"In case of what?"

In case he turns into a zombie and wants the first big brain he sees. This way he'll trip and won't be able to chase us.

"We're not creating a zombie. The spell should wake him up long enough to answer a couple questions. That's it. Then he's dead again." I hoped.

He's not wearing shoes anyway. Maybe I should tie his ankles together. Are you wearing a belt, by any chance?

"Please get down."

Raoul dropped to the floor and joined me a safe distance away. With the candles lit, there was no longer a need for the flashlight. The soft glow of the flames created dancing shadows on the plain white walls. I suddenly felt less alone.

I drew a deep breath and read the spell for what seemed like the hundredth time. If this went wrong, it could go *very* wrong. I pictured the judgmental faces of Hazel and Marigold slamming a door between us as they condemned me to a magic-free cell for eternity. I shook my head and cleared the images. I seemed to be mixing up Ivy's fate with my current reality.

I realized my palms were sweating. I wiped them on my pants and focused on my magic. Once upon a time, I would simply call to my magic, and it would rise up to meet me. If I did that now, I risked being swallowed by a tidal wave of magic. I had to be more careful—use a scalpel instead of a mallet. It didn't suit my personality, but I tried to view it through the lens of personal growth.

The magic coiled inside me, and I focused on the precise thread that I needed. Only what the spell required. Nothing more. I held onto what I needed and let the rest fall away. It took patience, which was not one of my virtues.

Once I had only the specific magic threads, I concentrated on unwinding them and sending them to the body of Bertram Lapp. I opened my palm to see shiny tendrils of magic, as dark as obsidian. I brought my hand closer to my mouth and *blew*.

Ribbons the color of midnight undulated through the air as if in slow motion. There was something mesmerizing about their rhythmic motion. They dispersed before they reached the corpse. I felt a release of pressure that I hadn't noticed building. It reminded me of when the clarity of sound returned, but I hadn't realized my ears were clogged in the first place.

I observed the victim's body. Nothing changed. Not a flicker of movement.

"Mr. Lapp?" I asked hesitantly.

The corpse remained still.

I looked around the morgue in confusion. "I don't understand. The spell seemed to work." There was no mistaking the presence of magic.

It definitely did something. Even I felt that. Raoul scampered across the floor and stood on his hind legs to sniff the corpse.

"What are you doing? Do you think he'll suddenly smell better?"

I want to see if his scent is different. Raoul dropped to all fours. *It isn't.* He gagged as he scurried back to me. *Maybe it takes a minute to take effect.*

"Maybe." We waited. The body didn't stir. "This is disappointing."

"It certainly is," a deep voice said.

The lights flickered on, startling me. I turned to see Deputy Bolan towering over us. I couldn't wait for the spell to break simply so that I didn't have to repeat the experience of being looked down upon by a leprechaun. It disturbed the natural order of things.

"How can you be so stealthy with feet that big?" I demanded.

"I have a more pressing question," Bolan began.

I popped to my feet. "What are you doing here at this hour?"

"Yes, that's the question," Bolan said.

"No, I was asking you," I replied.

He sensed a disturbance in the force, Raoul said.

"Security reported unusual activity in the morgue. I thought maybe Howard Lapp had decided not to wait until morning."

"I didn't realize the morgue was monitored."

"The healer uses a ward to detect motion."

Raoul tugged my pant leg. *See? The healer worries about zombies too.*

"You'd better blow out these candles right now. You've created a fire hazard."

Raoul ran to each wick and snuffed it out.

Bolan's gaze shifted from the candles to the corpse. "Don't tell me you were trying to revive him. Did you really think solving the case would be that easy? Wake up a dead guy and ask who killed him?" He clucked his tongue. "You've been doing this long enough to know better, Rose."

"It was worth a shot," I argued. "We're getting desperate."

"No, *you're* getting desperate. I have every confidence we'll catch the killer without disrespecting the victim." He walked across the room and pushed the slab into the locker.

"How is it disrespectful to want to help identify his killer?"

"It's disrespectful to disturb his peace in order to achieve it. Besides, you know how these things work. There's always a price that you wouldn't have offered to pay if you'd known up front." He shook his head. "I wouldn't have expected you to do a thing like this."

I stuffed the candles into the backpack with undue force. "You don't have to sound so disappointed."

Bolan wasn't ready to back off. "Do you have any idea how dangerous this is? What if you'd succeeded? How would you explain to Lapp's sons how we identified the killer? It's invasive and immoral. A real violation."

Raoul hung his head in shame.

I zipped the backpack and slung it over my shoulder. "You're right. I'm sorry."

The deputy scrutinized me. "Sorry you did it, or sorry you got caught?"

Now I was *really* having flashbacks of my misspent youth.

"I think it's time to pull you off the case," he continued.

My head jerked up. "What? No. Please don't do that."

I have mouths to feed, Raoul added. *Okay, only one mouth, but I eat so much that it's basically plural.*

I shot him a quizzical look before turning my attention back to the angry deputy.

"Deputy Pitt and I will handle the murder investigation from here."

My stomach lurched. "No. I can do this, Bolan. I don't know what possessed me to try necromancy. It won't happen again, I swear." I should've listened to Veronica. The seer told me that my magic would wreak havoc, but I failed to heed her warning. To be fair, I only ignored it because I thought she sensed Ivy's power, and it made her uncomfortable. Veronica had performed enough readings for me in the past that the intensity of magic would've felt unfamiliar to her.

"I can't allow it, Rose, and I don't think the sheriff would either if he could speak, no matter how he feels about you."

If Granger weren't stuck in his wolf form, none of this would likely be happening in the first place. I wisely didn't give voice to that thought. I'd ticked off Bolan enough for one night. I had no issue pushing leprechaun Bolan's buttons, but Buff Bolan was another story. What if, like Alec, he started to act the way he looked? I'd find myself on one of the open slabs.

"You're shorthanded, no pun intended." I swore loudly. I couldn't even rely on leprechaun puns right now. This spell had to end. "At least let me pursue the caster while you pursue the killer."

"Assuming they aren't one and the same," Bolan said.

I held up a hand as though swearing an oath. "I'll stick to leads pertaining to the spell and only the spell."

Silence stretched as Deputy Bolan regarded me. "Fine,"

he finally said. "Clean up your mess, and I'll lock up behind us. How did you get in here anyway?"

I wiggled my fingers. He looked at them without comment.

Raoul and I fled the building in silent humiliation.

We've had better days, Raoul commented, as I drove past Thornhold on our way to Rose Cottage.

"Sweet baby Elvis. There's Aunt Hyacinth." I almost ducked until I remembered I was the driver. Instead, I waved.

Where's she headed in the middle of the night? A romantic rendezvous with that wizard?

"I think Craig is out of the picture." I thought my aunt was moving at a glacial pace with the wizard. Eventually, it became clear that the relationship had reached an end, and in typical Hyacinth fashion, she hadn't seen fit to inform anybody. There was only one other reason she'd be out of the house at this hour. "It must be the Council of Elders meeting."

I parked outside Rose Cottage. Raoul unbuckled his seatbelt. *Must be almost midnight. You know what that means.*

"It's past my bedtime?"

Time for a midnight snack.

"I don't have much."

He offered a dismissive grunt. *I'm not raiding your fridge. I want quality. I'm heading to the dumpster at Feast.*

I watched as the raccoon ran toward the woods. I stood outside for a few minutes, debating my next move. Part of me wanted nothing more than to roll into bed and fall into a deep sleep. There was another part of me that felt too energized from the spell at the morgue to settle down just yet.

I glanced at Thornhold, the gears turning in my mind.

No doubt the Council of Elders would discuss the current situation. I swiveled to contemplate the cottage. Marley and PP3 were asleep. There was no harm in staying out a bit longer. I grabbed my cloak from the back seat of the car and headed to the stables. It was time to get back on the horse.

Chapter Seventeen

The meeting of the Council of Elders was a grand affair for an event that took place in a damp cave. There was the moonlight ride on horseback through the forest. The secrecy. The elite status of those involved. The flaming torches. I knew I was pushing boundaries turning up without an invitation, but the council was comprised of different species, which made it the ideal group to mine for information. My aunt was likely too proud to ask for help on behalf of the coven. She'd want the council to believe the coven had the mirror spell well in hand, whereas I had no problem admitting defeat. Aunt Hyacinth had a tendency to go to great lengths to keep up appearances. It was probably written in her will that, when she died, I was to prop her up *Weekend at Bernie's* style and pretend she was still alive and thriving. To be dead was to admit defeat.

I tethered the white horse to a live oak not far from the cave. "I'll be back soon," I told Candle. The horse whinnied gently in response.

I crept toward the entrance to the cave, straining to listen to the conversation underway.

"I won't tolerate the view any longer," Victorine Del Bianco's voice echoed. "Tell your shifter to take it down or suffer the consequences."

I inched forward.

"I'll do nothing of the sort. There's no ordinance that prohibits it," Arthur Rutledge replied in defense of his pack member. His voice was softer and more controlled.

"No one needs a twenty-foot-tall blow-up doll in their front yard," Victorine snapped.

"It isn't a blow-up doll," Arthur replied calmly. "It's an inflatable tube man."

I tiptoed further inside the cave. It seemed like an awkward moment to announce my presence. I decided to wait until the argument finished.

"It's an eyesore," Victorine shot back.

"So is that outfit you're wearing, but you don't hear anyone demanding you take it off," Arthur said.

"Good gods, no," someone else muttered.

Okay, *now* was a good time to interrupt, before the discussion became more heated.

"Excuse me," I said, stepping into view. "Is there room for one more?"

Aunt Hyacinth gave me a withering look. "Yarrow, what on earth are you doing here without an invitation?"

"Ember," I corrected her. "I'm hoping to bring up urgent new business, if the council will permit me."

"We're not at new business yet." Victorine lifted her chin, appraising me. "Where do you stand on inflatable yard ornaments?"

"Nowhere near them."

The vampire waved a hand at the stone table. "You may sit."

The cave was chillier than I anticipated, and I wished I'd brought a second layer. I planted myself safely between Misty Brookline and Amaryllis Elderflower, careful to avoid close proximity to my aunt. The closer I sat to her, the more I'd absorb her hostile energy.

"This rock is going to give me a butt cramp," I mumbled.

Misty tilted to the side to reveal the travel cushion beneath her bottom. "Next time," she whispered.

The argument switched to a new topic that was apparently still old business. I waited patiently, although the conversation was mind-numbingly boring.

"Is it new business yet?" I blurted. I could feel Aunt Hyacinth's glare from across the stone table. So much for staying in her good graces.

"I think we're ready to move on," Misty said.

Oliver Dagwood shifted toward me. "Now, Ember, what is it you'd like to discuss?" At first glance, the wizard appeared normal, until I spotted the tangle of nose hairs embedded in his generous nostrils.

"The mirror spell," I told them.

"That wretched spell," Amaryllis grumbled. "Yes, let's try to get to the bottom of it, please. I've had quite enough of it."

It was only then that I noticed her face. The long and narrow nose gave her the look of an exotic bird. I could understand her strong desire to undo the magic.

"I don't mind the spell," Mervin O'Malley said. The leprechaun seemed to have followed Bolan's lead. Although his skin was still the shade of a cucumber, he was as tall as his council counterparts.

"Some of us didn't fare so well," Misty interjected. The fairy's wings were covered by her yellow cloak, so I wasn't sure whether she'd lost hers like Bertram. Even in the dim light, however, I could see the worsening signs of age on her weathered face, and the way her hands trembled as they rested on the stone table. It seemed that Misty saw herself as old and frail.

"The coven wasn't able to reverse it," I said, "and we're no closer to identifying the caster. I thought we could brainstorm for a solution together."

"I don't see why you're in such a hurry to break the spell," Mervin said. "At least you've got an easy solution. There's hair dye for that, you know."

"Is that from the spell?" my aunt asked. "I thought you'd done that on purpose."

"Why would I do this to myself on purpose?" I swatted at my hair.

"It must be because you see yourself more as a Rose now," my aunt said, sounding pleased.

"It is a mirror spell, after all," Oliver interrupted. "Why not take the time to reflect on what the magic has revealed about your internal beliefs? If nothing else, it's a useful tool for personal growth."

"Yes, growth," I murmured, averting my gaze from his nose hairs.

"If the council had information that would help the sheriff's office, we would've brought it to their attention already," my aunt said.

There were murmurs of assent.

"Is it true Sheriff Nash is stuck in his werewolf form?" Misty asked.

"Sadly, yes," Arthur answered before I could. "He isn't the only werewolf to suffer this way. Maynard Howell is trapped in wolf form, too, only his wolf is as small as a pup."

"Inferiority complex," Mervin coughed into his hand.

"Takes one to know one," Victorine said smoothly.

Mervin glowered at her.

The vampire gave him a cool look. "You don't intimidate me at any size, O'Malley."

"That's enough," Amaryllis said. "I think we should at least entertain the question. What else is a council for if not to discuss matters that impact Starry Hollow?"

"It isn't only a matter of appearances," Victorine said. "I have at least one vampire in a protective chamber. He seems to think he's as feral as he looks."

It seemed Alec wasn't the only vampire to have that response to the spell.

"Do you have any leads at all, Ember?" Arthur asked.

"None that have panned out," I admitted. "I've focused on magic users with the skill level required, and those who've been expelled or sanctioned for an inappropriate use of magic."

"And how many of those are there?" Victorine asked.

"Not many, which is part of the problem." I paused. "Well, a problem in this case. Generally speaking, it's a good thing we don't have many."

"Because we rule with a firm hand," my aunt said.

"We don't rule at all," Misty countered. "We simply keep an eye on the town. Sheriff Nash deserves the credit for keeping law and order. He's a wonderful sheriff."

"Except when he's incapable of performing his duties, like now," Victorine said. Vampires and werewolves were forever at odds, it seemed, even when there was no reason to be.

"He's working closely on the case," I assured them. "He and I have a shorthand way of communicating."

Victorine smirked. "No doubt."

"What about Olga Rook-Nightshade?" Amaryllis asked. "The one who owns the pig farm. Wasn't she a troublemaker back in the day, Hyacinth?"

"I spoke to Olga," I said, "and we've ruled her out as a suspect. She doesn't use magic anymore."

"A shame," Amaryllis said. "She was quite talented, from what I recall."

Aunt Hyacinth sat up straighter. "What about her protégé? Did you speak to her?"

"That's right. Olga mentioned a witch she used to tutor. What was her name?" I drummed my fingers on the cool slab of stone.

Oliver snapped his fingers. "A wisp of a girl. What was her name?"

"It was Edith," Amaryllis said.

"No, it was Enid Marsh-Thorn," my aunt chimed in. "I used to play bridge with her grandmother before she died. Limoncello was a master at cards."

I opened my mouth to comment on the name but decided against it. Now wasn't the time for mockery, no matter how many jokes bubbled to the surface.

"If Enid is one of yours, why would she not speak up when you tried to reverse the spell?" Victorine asked, looking at my aunt.

"Because Enid isn't in the coven," Aunt Hyacinth replied.

"Expelled?" Arthur asked.

"No. She left of her own accord. As far as I know, she still resides in Starry Hollow. It should be easy enough to find her."

I looked across the table at my aunt. "She left voluntarily, and you let her?"

"That isn't an option for you, if that's what you're thinking," my aunt said. Unfortunately for me, Hyacinth Rose-Muldoon was every bit as smart as she looked. "Enid was a timid creature and not very adept at magic. Olga was asked to tutor her. I believe she was upset after the incident with Olga and chose to part ways with us."

"Wasn't Limony Snicket upset about that?" I asked.

"Limoncello was dead by then, thank the Goddess of the Moon. She would've been appalled to see what had become of her line."

"It doesn't sound as though Enid has the type of skill necessary to produce a spell of this magnitude," Amaryllis said.

"What about fairies?" Mervin asked. "Have you interviewed any of them?"

Aunt Hyacinth made a dismissive sound at the back of her throat that, if anybody else had done it, would've been described as "unladylike."

"I've spoken to a few fairies in connection with the murder of Bertram Lapp," I said vaguely. I didn't want to get into a magical pissing contest.

"Fairies wouldn't have the kind of power required to cast a spell like this," my aunt sniffed. "The culprit must be a wizard or witch."

Misty lifted her chin in protest. "I've known many a fairy capable of widespread magic, Hyacinth."

My aunt shifted her penetrating gaze to the unfortunate fairy. "Could *you* perform such a spell?"

Misty seemed to fold in on herself. "I don't know. Perhaps. It isn't the sort of thing I'd think to try."

"Maybe it was an accident," Mervin suggested. "Could be a fairy that didn't know their own strength."

"You've cracked the case, Mervin," my aunt said without a hint of humor. "My niece will simply round up every fairy in town for interrogation."

The leprechaun's glare sent daggers in her direction. "We're brainstorming, aren't we? I think suggesting that the spell was accidental falls into that category."

"We're still uncertain whether the spell was deliberate," I admitted.

"Then what *are* you sure of?" Arthur asked.

My gaze lowered to the table. "That Bertram Lapp was murdered, and there's a mirror spell that needs to break by sundown tomorrow or the effects might be permanent."

A collective gasp followed.

"It's only a theory," I added hastily.

"I don't see how Ember and the deputies could be expected to interview every incompetent magic user in town," Victorine said.

"There are three of them to conduct interviews," Arthur piped up. "Divide and conquer, I say."

I wanted to offer the same advice about his nose hairs.

Misty leaned over to me and whispered, "You might want to pay a visit to Kelsey Harper. You can find her at the roller rink."

"Skater?"

"Owner."

I knew better than to ask any further follow-up questions. Misty had whispered the suggestion for a reason.

"We might want to consider a protective ward that prevents this sort of thing from happening in the future," Victorine said.

"A ward around the whole town?" Mervin asked in disbelief.

I turned my focus to my aunt. "Is that even possible?"

"The coven could certainly generate the power required for such a ward."

"Then why haven't we done it already?" Mervin asked, his thick eyebrows drawn together in suspicion.

"Because of unforeseen consequences," Aunt Hyacinth replied. "What if Starry Hollow is attacked, and we want to cast a town-wide spell to arm everyone with magic?"

"In the unlikely event that happens," Victorine began, "couldn't you break the ward and then cast the spell?"

"Time would be of the essence in such a situation," my aunt said.

"I'm thinking that's a pretty far-fetched scenario," I said. "You might want to consider the ward."

Aunt Hyacinth's eyes burned with annoyance. "It isn't the only scenario. It's simply one example."

"There's already a ward that conceals the town from the human world," I said. "Couldn't you just add another layer to that magic?" Although I didn't know the right terminology, that was how I pictured it in my mind.

"It can certainly be a topic for discussion at the next coven meeting," my aunt said, "but right now, I think it's best to focus on the current situation, given the sense of urgency."

I agreed. "If anybody thinks of another potential caster, you know how to reach me."

Oliver regarded me with interest. "I think the spell brought out your confidence, Ember. There's a light in you I haven't noticed before."

"Nonsense," my aunt cut in. "Ember has always exuded confidence. She's a Rose."

My thoughts turned to Linnea, who thought so little of herself that she actually became little, but I said nothing.

"I see what you mean, Oliver," Amaryllis said, leaning back to study me. "Her aura shimmers. Interesting, isn't it?"

I suddenly felt uncomfortable. I didn't like being put under a magical microscope.

"You can go now, Ember," my aunt said. There was no mistaking the note of dismissal in her voice.

"Thank you for letting me interrupt your meeting," I said. *A Rose must always remember her courtesies.*

I pulled up the hood of my cloak as I emerged from the mouth of the cave. I heard Candle's unsettled noises before the horse came into view. Something—or someone—was upsetting the horse. I'd left the backpack in the car, so I didn't have any magical accessories with me. Still, I crept through the trees toward the horse to see what was spooking my ride. My heart hammered in my chest as the horse's discomfort grew louder. I wondered whether I'd see the same visions as before. Supernatural bonfires and shadowy figures would certainly be enough to spook even the calmest and collected horse. I wasn't sure when the forest became haunted, but I voted for an immediate exorcism.

Amber eyes flashed in the darkness, and I froze in place. They didn't belong to one of the earlier visions, but they didn't promise a positive encounter either unless...

"Granger?" I whispered.

The wolf stepped into the patch of moonlight, and I breathed a sigh of relief. Tipping back my hood, I kneeled down to greet him.

"What are you doing here? Did you follow me?"

The wolf licked my hand.

I glanced over at the horse. "It's all right, Candle," I said in a soothing tone. "It's only Granger."

The horse whinnied and stopped shuffling.

I buried my face in the wolf's soft fur. "I miss you too. Apparently ,my moral compass goes on the fritz without your steady hand to guide me. I won't even tell you what I tried to do earlier." Although I was sure Bolan would.

The wolf howled. The lonely sound cut through the thick silence of the forest.

"I swear I'm going to fix this." I couldn't risk the accuracy of Veronica's claim that if the spell didn't break by sundown tomorrow, everyone would be trapped in their new forms forever. I owed it to Granger—to everyone—to keep trying.

The wolf turned and started toward the cottage. It seemed he wanted to spend the night at Rose Cottage again, not that I blamed him. He probably felt so isolated and alone right now.

I mounted Candle, making sure to maintain a safe distance behind the wolf so as not to frighten the horse. We traveled through the woods without incident. No spectral visions or unnerving noises. I returned the horse safely to the stables. By the time I reached the cottage, exhaustion had set in. Granger seemed to be on the same page because he shot upstairs and curled up on the bed. I curled against his warm fur and said a silent prayer to the gods that tomorrow would be a better day.

Chapter Eighteen

The next morning Granger's side of the bed was empty. I dragged myself downstairs to cook breakfast for Marley before school. I'd been hoping to feed Granger, too, but there was no sign of the wolf.

"Did you let Granger out?" I asked, cracking eggs into a bowl.

"He's not a dog. He must've let himself out."

"He has paws, not opposable thumbs," I pointed out. I heard a satisfying hiss as the eggs made contact with the hot pan.

"Yes, but he still has Granger's brain." She looked at me and frowned. "Did you have nightmares again?"

"Late night." I used magic to heat the bacon and cut down on grease splatter. I scrambled the eggs and added them to the plate with the bacon. The aroma would probably lure Raoul from whatever dumpster he'd slept in. "What makes you think I've been having nightmares?" I passed her a plate of eggs and bacon.

Marley ducked her head and focused intently on her food. "Oops. I told myself I wasn't going to say anything."

I sat in the chair adjacent to hers. "Tell me."

"You've been crying, yelling." She paused to drink water from her glass. "I've checked on you a couple times when it sounded pretty bad. You thrash around in your bed, then settle down again. I thought maybe you scared Granger away this time."

"I think it would take a lot more than that to scare him away." Granger had shown me that he was here to stay, which was one of the many reasons I loved him. "I'm sorry I've been waking you. I didn't realize."

"It's okay. I fall right back to sleep." She smiled. "Besides, how many times have I woken you up over the years? It's payback time, I guess."

"No, payback time will be when I'm an old insomniac living in your spare bedroom."

She shrugged. "That doesn't sound as horrible to me as it probably should."

I ruffled her hair. "That's because you love me." I returned to the stovetop to cook my own breakfast.

"What's on your agenda today?" Marley asked.

"I'll be starting my day at the roller rink."

Marley choked on her eggs. "Don't you think you're a little old for that?"

"Mind your tongue, miss." I made a threatening gesture with the spatula. "I have a lead on the mirror spell. Two leads, in fact."

I'd only been to the roller rink once when Marley had attended a birthday party not long after we arrived in Starry Hollow. She'd spent the entire two hours waving to kids from the sidelines, too fearful to put on skates.

"Don't hurt yourself," Marley said. "Your balance isn't the best when you're wearing shoes. I can't imagine what it's like on wheels."

She wasn't wrong. "What's on your agenda today?"

"Pop quiz in my first class."

I squinted at her. "Isn't a pop quiz a surprise?"

"It is, but Keenan has precognition, so he tells our study group when to expect any unannounced quizzes."

"Isn't that dangerously close to cheating?" I joined her at the table with my plate of food. She immediately reached for one of my bacon strips, and I gently smacked away her hand.

"I've asked him to stop telling me, but he blurts it out. It's almost like a tic."

"Magical Tourette's," I remarked.

"It isn't like I need advanced warning anyway. I have a perfect grade in the class, mainly because I keep getting one wrong, but then I get the bonus question right." She shrugged.

"I almost forgot to ask—how was your meetup at the coffee shop?"

Her cheeks turned bright pink. "Good. Lots of kids were there."

"Sounds fun." I didn't want to prod for more information. I'd let her tell me in her own time.

She glanced at the clock. "Time to go. I'm staying after school to work on a science project, but I'll be home for dinner."

I kissed her cheek. "Okay. Have a great day." I demolished the bacon on my plate. All that magic yesterday had made me ravenous.

Once I was showered and dressed, I debated whether to wait for Raoul. In the end, I decided to go to the roller rink on my own. Knowing the raccoon, he'd insist on finding a pair of skates in his size.

I swung by Caffeinated Cauldron for a latte with a shot

of promise and continued by car to the rink. Retro Rollers was located near an industrial complex on the outskirts of town. Although the rink wasn't open for customers at this hour, the door was unlocked, so I let myself in.

"Hello? Anybody here?" I called.

Despite the early hour, the rink was illuminated by bold flashing colors. I had to avert my gaze before the lights gave me a blinding headache.

"Can I help you?" a voice asked.

I turned around and was met by a young fairy. Her hair was covered in purple ringlets and her golden wings glistened in the light. There was something oddly familiar about her face, but I couldn't quite place it.

"Are you Kelsey Harper?"

The fairy smiled. "That's me. If you want to skate, you'll have to wait until ten. That's when we open."

I laughed. "Oh, I am definitely not here to skate."

"If you're selling something..." She frowned. "Wait. I know you. Amber Rose, isn't it?"

"Ember." I presented her with my business card.

"Hmm," she said, reading the card. "Personally, I would've gone with Amber. At least then you'd get to be pretty and golden instead of a pile of ash."

"Could be worse," I said. "I could be Yarrow."

Kelsey grimaced. "Good heavens. Who would name a baby Yarrow?"

As long as we were on the same page with Yarrow, I opted to forgive her initial insult.

"I've seen you around town," Kelsey continued. "You have the cutest familiar. Makes me wish I were a witch instead of a fairy."

"I'll be sure to tell him you said so," I lied. There was no way I could tell Raoul, or I'd never hear the end of it.

"I think I'd like to have a hedgehog," she said, "as my familiar, I mean."

"I hate to break it to you, but you don't get a choice."

"Oh, that's a shame. Then how did you end up with a raccoon?"

"Raoul is a gift from the gods," I said, injecting an air of mystery into the statement. Aunt Hyacinth would beg to differ. She considered Raoul to be an embarrassing anomaly that must've come from my mother's gene pool.

Kelsey's shoulders slumped. "I wish I had a gift from the gods. Then maybe I wouldn't be such a failure."

"Why would you say that? Don't you own this place?"

"Yes, as a matter of fact I do own this money pit." She grimaced. "I'd originally planned to own a salon, but I flunked out of cosmetology school. I kept turning blue hair red and adding stripes to wings instead of glitter." She laughed. "I was a disaster."

"You should've seen me when I first moved to Starry Hollow. I had a stable of tutors, yet I still messed up every spell I was assigned."

"I'm sure Hyacinth loved that," Kelsey said. "That's a joke, by the way. I've met your aunt enough times to know she would not appreciate a flawed performance."

Oddly enough, I felt compelled to come to my aunt's defense. "She's softened over time."

Kelsey grunted. "I guess there's hope for anyone, in that case. My aunt Misty isn't nearly as domineering as Hyacinth, but I can still tell she wishes I were more adept at magic. I could feel her secondhand embarrassment when I flunked out of school."

"Misty Brookline is your aunt?" I hadn't realized. No wonder the older fairy hadn't been willing to suggest Kelsey's name to the rest of the council. She was being a protective aunt. I was familiar with the type.

"She's my father's older sister. Everyone on that side of the family is high achieving. I wouldn't say I'm the black sheep, but I definitely get listed last on family Christmas cards."

"I was such a black sheep that I got raised in a different pasture."

Kelsey's gaze slid to my head. "Yes, I see that, although you do have a few telltale streaks. Have you considered going full white-blond to blend in with the rest of your family? With your pale skin, I bet you'd look good."

I touched my hair. "You think the streaks are blond?" I assumed the mirror spell had given me white strands because I was starting to feel old, but maybe Aunt Hyacinth had been right—maybe they were actually white-blond because I was starting to feel more like a real Rose instead of an imposter.

Kelsey studied my hair. "Looks white-blond to me. I guess it's hard to tell when it's against such a dark background." She cocked her head. "Did the spell do that to you?"

I nodded. "The spell is actually the reason I'm here."

"Oh, is the coven doing welfare checks? That makes sense. I have to imagine some residents are really in bad shape. Even a spell that makes someone look old can wreak havoc on their psyche."

"Some are definitely worse off than others," I agreed.

"Is it true someone died because of the spell? Because I agree that guy is way worse off."

"A fairy named Bertram Lapp died when the spell took hold. We're not sure at this point whether it's a coincidence."

"Lapp," she repeated. "That's a fairy family."

"Yes. Two sons, Jeremiah and Timothy. A cousin named Howard."

Her face darkened. "I didn't realize it was Timothy's dad who died. That's terrible."

"You know Timothy?"

"We played in a band together for a few months when their bass player broke his arm. I may be garbage at magic, but I'm excellent on the guitar." She wiggled her fingers. "I play here on Tuesdays and Thursdays for '80s party nights."

"Sounds fun. Which instrument does Timothy play?"

"Drums. I suspect they help him channel all that energy."

Energy—or rage? "Do you think Timothy is capable of violence?"

Kelsey's hesitation answered my question. "I think a lot of us are capable of violence. It's whether we act on it, right?"

"Sounds like Timothy might have issues with impulse control."

"Yeah, he's the opposite of his brother. Jeremiah's wound so tight, Timothy used to say he lost one of his drumsticks up..." She trailed off. "Never mind. It's crude."

"Do you like Timothy?"

"Yeah, he isn't so bad. He doesn't have a lot to say, but that's not necessarily a negative. Some paranormals don't know when to keep quiet. Timothy strikes me as a fairy who wants a life of simple pleasures."

I thought about the victim's will and the family orchard. "Did he ever complain about a lack of money?"

"No, he didn't seem very interested in money. I mean, he wanted to earn enough to get by, but he wasn't concerned with status or material goods. Even his drum set was secondhand, but he loved it."

"Did he ever talk about his dad?"

"Not often. His parents showed up at a few gigs, and I remember Timothy being happy about that. His parents' support was important to him." She frowned. "It must be hard for him now, losing both parents."

I knew from experience how hard it was. "At least he still has his brother." I didn't even have that much.

"He and Jeremiah are too different to be close. Jeremiah refused to come to any gigs because he didn't like the music we played. He called it 'garbage noise.'"

"That wasn't very kind."

Kelsey shrugged. "That's brothers, I guess."

"Stories like that make me glad to be an only child."

"You and me both." She sighed. "Although I always wondered what it would be like to have a sister. I like watching the rink on Family Night. You see the older siblings holding the younger one's hand. It's so sweet."

I gazed at the bright lights of the rink and imagined the skaters circling the surface. It was the kind of place I would've begged my dad to bring me when I was a kid. It didn't matter that I knew I'd fall over fifty times. I wanted to have the experience, mostly because it was an excuse to hold my dad's hand.

"Which night is Family Night?" I asked.

"Wednesdays. It's 6 p.m. to 8 p.m. to accommodate the younger ones."

I made a mental note. I suddenly had a strong urge to return with Marley. I shouldn't have let her sit on the sidelines back then. I should've taken her by the hand, like my dad had done for me.

"I take it you didn't come here for a skating schedule," Kelsey said.

"No, to be honest, I came to ask whether you cast the mirror spell."

The fairy stared at me, wide eyed. "Are you for real?" She doubled over with laughter. "You're a hoot, Ember." Standing upright again, she wiped tears from her eyes. "By the gods, you are serious."

"Afraid so."

"If I had that kind of power, do you think I would've been kicked out of cosmetology school?"

"You didn't get booted for lack of power. You got booted for lack of control."

She regarded me. "I see. So someone with power but no control might've cast a spell that inadvertently affected the whole town."

"Exactly."

Kelsey shook her purple ringlets. "It wasn't me, sorry. My magic is limited to lights, camera, and action." She motioned to the rink.

"No one's asked you to perform magic for them, have they? Maybe offered you money?"

"Nobody in their right mind would do that. And if they did, they'd have to be a complete stranger. If you know anything about me at all, you know I'm a pimple on the nose of magic."

I laughed. "I think you're underestimating yourself. The rink looks amazing. If you're fueling this with your magic, you're better than you believe."

Despite her obvious abilities, I trusted my intuition that Kelsey had nothing to do with the mirror spell.

"Now you sound like Aunt Misty," Kelsey said. "She's

always saying things like that. 'You need to see yourself as you truly are, Kelsey. If you don't, nobody else will either.'"

"Maybe it's time to believe her."

Kelsey's eyes grew moist as her expression softened. "Maybe it is."

Chapter Nineteen

I crossed Kelsey Harper off my list and moved on to the second lead I'd been given by the council—Olga's protégé, Enid Marsh-Thorn. A quick call to Bentley revealed that Enid was, in fact, still local and owned a small perfume company called Whiff.

"I can't believe you haven't been there," the elf scolded me. "Her fragrances are legendary in Starry Hollow. I bought Meadow a bottle there for her birthday last month."

"Consider me educated." I paused, debating whether to ask my next question. In the end, I couldn't help myself. "How's Alec? Did he come back to the office?"

"How did you know about that?"

"I ran into him by the deli. He was a mess."

"He seems better now. I mean, he still looks like a creature from the black lagoon, but he seems to have gotten the rest of himself in check. I'm going to go out on a limb and guess that was your influence."

"I'm glad he's back at the office." Work was Alec's safe space. It must've been hard on him to be cut off from his needs.

"I hope this spell breaks soon," Bentley complained. "If I have to see Tanya take one more selfie, I'm going to puke."

"Let her enjoy it while it lasts."

"What about you? Have you grown devil horns or anything cool?"

I frowned at the phone. "Why would I have grown devil horns?"

"No reason." He cleared his throat. "Oh, look. A call on my other line. Gotta go. Byeeee."

I set down the phone and drove to the address he'd given me for Whiff. With its downtown location, I was surprised I hadn't noticed it before.

I entered the building and immediately spotted the sign for Enid's office at the far end. Between us, however, was a maze of sleek glass counters and shelves lined with equally sleek perfume bottles. In the middle of the maze was a minotaur holding a bottle, clearly angling to spritz me with a sample. Our eyes locked, and I bolted to the left. Ahead of me the office sign loomed like a beacon in the night. The layout of the counters lost the minotaur precious moments. I ducked behind a tall display and continued to walk at a brisk pace, fighting the urge to sprint the rest of the way. My heart pounded when I realized I'd lost sight of her. I peeked around the side of the display. There was no sign of the minotaur.

I began to relax. Enid's office was within reach. As I started forward, the minotaur stepped directly into my path, holding the elegant perfume bottle.

"Welcome to Whiff. Would you like to try our signature fragrance?" Bam! She spritzed me right in the face. I started coughing, prompting the minotaur to apologize profusely. "I didn't mean to press down yet. I am so sorry."

My eyes burned for a brief moment. When I finally

opened them, I could see the minotaur was on the verge of tears. With the boss's office right behind her, I understood her regret.

"I'm fine." I took a tissue from my purse and wiped my eyes. "It actually smells good."

She beamed at me. "Doesn't it? Whiff's own secret formula."

"It's earthy. I prefer that to a floral scent."

She clutched the bottle to her chest. "Me too! My boyfriend loves this one. He's a centaur, so I think this kind of scent appeals to him."

"In that case, do you have one that smells like a slab of meat?"

Her eyes sparked with enthusiasm. "As a matter of fact, we do," she chirped. "It's called Raw. Would you like a free sample?"

I stared at her, gobsmacked. That was not the answer I expected. "Um, maybe later. Is your boss in?"

She glanced down at the bottle in her hand with disappointment. "You're not in the market for a fragrance?"

"Not today. Sorry."

"If you change your mind, my name's Lyssa. I'll be right over there next to the holiday collection." She motioned to the counter.

"That's early."

"We like to get shoppers in the spirit as soon as possible."

No doubt. I continued to the office door and knocked.

"What is it?" a voice snapped.

I cracked open the door and peered inside. The office interior was as elegant as the perfume bottle that had assaulted me. Enid sat behind a royal blue desk with gold leaf legs. Aunt Hyacinth would approve.

Enid was equally elegant. Her chestnut hair was worn in the French twist that my aunt favored. Her eye makeup was impeccable, just enough to accent her best feature without overdoing it. If I weren't here on business, I'd ask for tips—that I could pass along to Hazel.

"You're not Lisa." The witch's hard expression didn't change.

"I think her name is Lyssa."

"And?" Enid stared at me like I had two heads. "How can I help you?"

I strode to the desk and placed my business card in front of her. "My name is Ember. I'd like to speak to you about a recent incident." I deliberately omitted my last name this time. Based on her behavior so far, she wouldn't bother to look at the business card either.

As Enid slotted her hands together, I counted three large gemstones on her rings. "And what incident is that?"

"A spell was cast that impacted most of the town."

She whistled through her pink lipstick. "Most of the town? That's impressive."

"It is," I agreed. "I'm working with the sheriff to find the caster."

She didn't blink. "Why? Are they in trouble?"

"Not if they reverse the spell." That wasn't strictly true, but I needed her to talk. "You can't possibly tell me you haven't heard about the mirror spell."

She assessed me coolly. "I've heard. I just wasn't sure whether that was the spell you meant. This is Starry Hollow, after all. Lots of magic flying around town on a daily basis."

Okay, we were playing games. Might as well get comfortable. I sat in the velvet-cushioned chair opposite her.

"We need to find the caster so we can turn everyone back into themselves."

"What makes you think they aren't themselves? As far as I understand it, the spell revealed the truth."

"What qualifies as the truth? I met a woman whose feet belong on a hobbit. Is that considered the truth because she believed her feet were larger than they are?"

Enid shrugged her narrow shoulders. "It's her truth."

"But that isn't always reality, is it? My daughter looks like a younger version of me, but that isn't reality either. Marley should look like herself."

Enid's posture became rigid. "You seem to be taking this personally. You might want to think about why that is." She patted a bottle on the edge of her desk. "Now, if you're finished, I'd like to get back to work. These fragrances aren't going to spray themselves."

Looking at the bottle, I suddenly remembered a comment Olga had made about the spell she'd used at the May Day dance.

She'd *sprayed* it into the air. Not the typical delivery system for a spell. No wonder it had impacted more than its intended target.

I pinned Enid with a hardened expression. "You cast the mirror spell, didn't you?"

Enid stared at me for a moment, and I saw the twitch in her eye the precise moment she decided to come clean. She threw up her hands. "Fine, it was me, but it wasn't supposed to affect the whole town. The spell turned out more potent than I realized."

"Because of the delivery system?"

Her sculpted eyebrows shot up. "Yeah. I think so." Her nails clicked on a bottle that rested on her desk. "The potion was sprayed into the air rather than ingested. I gave the client a portable atomizer bottle the size of a pen. They were instructed to spray the area of the target until the bottle was empty."

"How could something so small have such a wide impact?"

"I assume because it was spread via air molecules. I'd seen something similar happen once before."

"The May Day dance."

Enid smiled. "Someone's been doing her homework. The spray had been my idea. It's what gave me the idea to specialize in spelled fragrances."

"The effect was almost instantaneous though. It defies science."

She looked down her nose at me. "It's magic, darling. Of course it does."

How could someone as inept as Enid allegedly was craft a spell as powerful as this one? "I was under the impression that you weren't very good at magic. That's why you were being tutored by Olga."

Enid's eyes blazed with anger and indignation. "That was years ago. I've bloomed since then. I poured all my energy into learning perfume potions. Nobody in town does what I do at Whiff. I'm a trailblazer in the field."

And modest too. "And you created a custom potion for someone. Who's the client?"

She pursed her lips. "I can't tell you that."

"Why not? Did you miss the part where I said the sheriff is investigating the matter?"

"I can't tell you because I don't know. The client chose to remain anonymous."

"Did the client say why they wanted to cast a spell like this?"

"Not explicitly, no. I was given the general goal. My job was to craft a potion to achieve that goal."

"Which was?"

She folded her arms. "The potion was meant to open the target's eyes to see someone as they truly are."

But instead, the spell opened everyone's eyes to how they saw themselves. The spell had been intended to reveal someone's true nature to another—but whose and why?

"If your business is so successful, then why accept a side job?"

"I accept custom requests as part of my practice. I have a lab in the basement of this building where I develop all my fragrances, as well as any bespoke potions. The one thing they all have in common is that they're to be sprayed or spritzed, never swallowed."

"It didn't make you wary that the customer didn't want to identify themselves? Seems like a giant red flag to me."

She examined the tips of her French manicure. "Not necessarily. Certain types of paranormals get embarrassed when they need help from a magic user, especially if it's another magic user who simply doesn't have the skills required for the spell."

I squinted at her. "You think the mystery customer might be a member of the coven?"

"A magic user or a shifter. Shifters tend to resent the existence of magic in general, but they're still willing to look the other way when it suits them."

I could attest to that. When I'd first met Granger, one of the reasons he disliked my family was because of Aunt Hyacinth's lauded status in Starry Hollow due to her magical power and prestige, yet he was more than happy to accept magical help when it meant solving a case. It was simply the means to an end.

"How did they contact you?" I asked.

"Don't bother with that line of thought. The number doesn't work anymore. I sent a message back to thank them for their business and ask for a testimonial for my website, but it was no longer in service."

"How did they pay you?" Maybe I could trace the money to the source.

"Cash in an unsealed envelope, and I left the package in a place they'd designated behind the building."

"Was anything else in the package?"

"Only the portable atomizer."

I glanced around the room for any sign of a display monitor. "I don't suppose you have security cameras."

"No." She regarded me beneath a set of thick lashes. "Why are you so intent on the client if you only want to break the spell?"

"Because we believe the spell is linked to a murder."

Enid's brow furrowed. "You should've started with that part."

"We're not one hundred percent sure, but we think the timing is too great to ignore."

She frowned. "You don't think my spell is responsible, do you? I don't see how."

I decided not to sugarcoat it. "Indirectly, yes. At the very least, it acted as a distraction for the killer. At most, it aided the killer in accomplishing the task."

Her mouth formed a thin line. "You have no evidence of that."

"Not yet, but it's only a matter of time." I hoped. "At least help us break the spell so we can all get on with our lives."

She leaned back against her crushed velvet chair, assessing me. "And why would I want to do that? Some paranormals seem perfectly happy with their new appearance."

I ticked the reasons off on my fingers. "Because it's the right thing to do. Because it'll build goodwill between you and the coven. Because the sheriff will arrest you if you don't."

"Okay, that last reason is legitimate, but why would I care about the coven's goodwill? They didn't kick me out. I chose to leave after I saw how they treated Olga for one mistake. I thought if someone as competent as Olga could be shunned, what might they do to me when I inevitably displease them?"

As much as I wanted to argue, I couldn't find the words. In truth, I understood her position. I'd endured an unpleasant experience with the coven during my rift with Aunt Hyacinth.

"We're all flawed individuals, Enid, but that's not the worst part. The worst part is making a mistake and refusing to acknowledge it, instead of taking responsibility, holding yourself accountable, and offering a sincere apology."

Enid's nostrils flared. "I don't need the coven. I've done fine without them." She spread her arms wide. "I have a thriving business and more money than I'll ever need. I've become a leading expert in my field. That never would've happened if I hadn't strayed from the flock."

"And that's all you want out of life—money? Have you not seen *A Christmas Carol*?"

She glowered at me. "And who are you in that analogy—the Ghost of Past Mistakes? Newsflash, Ms. Rose. That mistake doesn't haunt me."

"But maybe it should." Either Enid was a sociopath, or she'd repressed any and all emotions connected to the spell as a coping mechanism. I really hoped it was the latter, for all our sakes.

Enid fiddled with a gold pen, tapping it incessantly against the desk. "I suppose you're a big deal in the coven. You probably sit at the special table right up front with your cousins."

"I do."

"When I was younger, I dreamed of becoming High Priestess one day. I'd play in the woods and lead my own ritual with my dolls. I was so crushed when they paired me with Olga for extra lessons. I felt ashamed and disappointed not to be the magical prodigy I longed to be. My grandmother would've been so disappointed."

"Be careful what you wish for. I happen to know of a magical prodigy, and I can tell you that things didn't work out so well for her."

Enid stopped tapping the pen. "Are you talking about your ancestor? The one who was stripped of her magic?"

"Ivy."

Her eyes shone. "Yes, that's right. The former High Priestess. I wrote a paper about her at the academy. I was obsessed with her for the longest time."

Where was Enid when I was conducting my own research on the ancient witch? "She had a tragic albeit fascinating life."

Enid looked at me with renewed interest. "You're very fortunate, Ms. Rose. You walked straight into a legacy."

I offered a rueful smile. "It doesn't always feel fortunate."

"If you have even a fraction of your ancestor's power, you should be able to break the spell yourself."

I'd considered it after the failed attempt by the coven, but Pollock's warning to Hazel put me off the idea. Like

Kelsey Harper, I had power but little control. With my luck, I'd literally turn everyone in town inside out. I didn't say any of this to Enid, of course.

"Wouldn't it be so much better if you simply volunteered your services?" I said. "It would be faster, plus it would give you the chance to heal old wounds. A win-win."

Enid's severe expression dissipated. "And what if I fail? The mirror spell didn't behave exactly as intended. I'm not certain I can break it even it if I want to."

There. Right there was the real reason for her hubris. Enid was using it to mask that same vulnerability she'd felt as a child.

"Enid, you said it yourself—you created a successful business and became a leading expert in your field. It seems to me that in your quest to prove your worth, you've become more powerful than even you realized." I leaned forward. "If anyone can break the spell, it isn't a Rose. It's you."

We stared at each other for what seemed like a full minute. She seemed to waver. I was afraid to speak and ruin the moment.

Enid was first to break the silence. "I'll consider it," was all she said.

I picked up her gold pen and scribbled my address on the back of the business card. "If you decide to take one for the team, meet me in the woods behind Rose Cottage before sunset."

Enid seemed to return to her hardened state. "Or what? You'll have me arrested? Not much of choice, is there?"

"I won't tell them yet. If you decide to show up, I won't even tell them it was you that cast the spell in the first place. I'll let you swoop in and play the hero."

Enid stared at me with narrowed eyes. "Why would you do that for me? You don't even know me."

"Because everyone deserves a second chance."

"Like Scrooge?"

"Like Scrooge. Like witches too big for their britches. Like brothers who don't pull their weight. Like women who make the wrong choice for the right reason."

She smirked. "Is that last one supposed to be you?"

I didn't want to confide in her about my rocky start with Granger. "Let's just say it all worked out for the best, but only because someone cared enough to give me a second chance."

Enid abruptly broke eye contact. "You've made your pitch, Ms. Rose. Now I have work to do. This successful business isn't going to run itself, no matter how much magic I have."

I'd done my best. The rest was up to her. "I'm glad I found you, Enid. I was beginning to think we'd be stuck like this forever." I rose to my feet. "See you tonight, I hope."

Enid didn't answer.

Chapter Twenty

I leaned to the side to see past the row of live oaks. The sun was beginning its descent, and there was no Enid in sight. As my doubts started to creep in, I swept them aside. *Enid's going to do the right thing*, I told myself.

You seem awfully optimistic about someone who created a fragrance called Raw Dog, Raoul said.

"It's just Raw."

I'd sequestered Granger in the cottage with Marley and Deputy Bolan with explicit instructions to await my signal. Well, not too explicit. I didn't tell them about Enid's role in the spell, only that I was trying another counterspell and wanted them nearby for confirmation of its success.

"Do you see Enid?" I asked.

Not since the last time you asked sixty seconds ago, Raoul replied.

I scanned the darkening horizon. The sun was about to set. A few more seconds and Granger might be a wolf forever. I didn't like those odds.

Someone's here, Raoul said excitedly.

A cloaked figure cut through the woods toward us. I

didn't need her to remove her cloak to know it was Enid. I could smell her scent from here. Light and floral.

She arrived at the clearing holding a leather tote bag. "You're really here alone?" She seemed surprised.

"I told you I wouldn't rat you out. This is my familiar, Raoul."

Enid glanced at the raccoon. "My familiar's an orange striped cat called Calliope." She opened the tote bag and produced an atomizer. The shiny red bottle looked like an oversized tube of lipstick. Somehow it seemed appropriate.

"That's the antidote?" I asked, or whatever it was called.

"I hope so. I worked for hours on it. I'm sure I look terrible."

I peered at her face and saw only the same exquisite makeup that I'd noticed in her office. "What do we do?"

"Spritz it in the air, same as the first one." She removed the lid and handed it to me. "Would you care to do the honors, Ms. Rose?"

"I think you should do it."

She continued to hold the bottle in front of me. "Why? You don't trust me?"

Enid's desire to pass the baton seemed to reflect her self-doubt. "I trust you, Enid, and I want you to trust yourself. You made the potion, and you should be the one to spritz it." I knew from my own experience that victory would taste sweeter if she handled the successful spell from start to finish.

Enid inhaled deeply. "Fine. Here goes nothing." She spritzed the potion, and we watched the droplets merge with the air. "Just watch. This time it'll actually work as a localized spell."

"How do you really think it spread so fast?" I asked. "And don't say magic."

She sighed. "But it *is* magic. I think the potion particles got picked up and carried through the town ley lines. You know how swift those currents can move, and they criss-cross the whole town."

I hadn't thought of that.

After a couple minutes, I sent a text to Marley in the cottage to check on their status, but she didn't respond.

Your hair hasn't changed back, Raoul said.

Darkness spread through the forest as the sun finally dipped below the horizon. So much for Veronica's prediction. My heart sank.

"Is there any left in the bottle?" I asked. "Maybe we should try more."

She shook the bottle. "That's the last of it. I engineered the delivery mechanism to work the same as the first one, so if that one managed to spread through the ether, then so should this one."

Desperation began to gnaw at me. "I bet there's a few drops left at the bottom. Can you just dump it out?"

"I don't think that'll be necessary," a familiar voice said.

I whirled around and found myself face to face with Granger in his human form. I threw my arms around him and clung to him like a barnacle to a sexy whale.

"How's my hair?" I asked.

"Hmm," Granger said.

I released him. "My hair still hasn't changed back?"

The werewolf cocked his head, staring at the top of my head. "I think the streaks are fading."

"Why wouldn't it be instantaneous like everyone else?" I twisted to look at Enid, but she was gone.

Yeah, she took off, Raoul confirmed. *Want me to chase her? That might be fun.*

No, let her go. I intended to keep my promise.

"You did it, Rose."

I looked down to see a very green and very petite Deputy Bolan. "Sorry about that, buddy."

The leprechaun shrugged. "I don't feel any different. As far as I'm concerned, I'm the same big deal I've always been."

I smiled. "That tracks." I thought of Alec and hoped that he was back to his handsome self, if for no other reason than I'd hate for him to ruin another suit.

Marley appeared behind him, also looking like herself again. "Linnea's grown back," she said. "I think everybody's normal again."

"How'd you do it, Rose?" Granger asked.

"I had professional help," I said vaguely.

"About time," Bolan muttered. "Well, one crisis down. One to go. I'm going to drive home and celebrate with my husband. Maybe this dinner will go uninterrupted."

Marley's phone jingled, and she read the screen. "Can I meet my friends at Caffeinated Cauldron? Everyone wants to compare changes."

"Okay, but..."

"I know. Take Bonkers." She whistled for her familiar, who landed on her shoulder.

Raoul fixed me with his beady eyes. *You two want to be alone now, don't you?*

That would be nice.

The raccoon groaned and followed Marley and Bolan out of the woods.

Granger swept the hair back from my face. "I've missed looking at you from this level."

"I've missed looking at you, period." I gazed at him. "Do you really see a wolf when you look in the mirror?"

"Not literally, but it's how I feel inside." He paused. "Not just a wolf. An animal."

I stroked his stubbled cheek with my thumb. "You say 'animal' like it's a bad thing."

He grabbed my hand and kissed it. "I see it as the lowest form of humanity, and that's not the kind of man I want to be."

I thought of Alec's monstrous version of himself. "I think your self-loathing needs improvement. You could've gone lower."

He wore a faint smile. "Only you would criticize the extent of my self-loathing."

"My aunt could probably give me a run for my money." The words that flew out of my mouth finally settled in my brain. "Sweet baby Elvis. Am I more like Aunt Hyacinth than I think?"

Granger wrapped me in a tight embrace. "You both speak your minds, but I think that's the most you have in common."

"Phew." I listened to his heartbeat inside his broad chest and felt my body relax. "I'm so glad you're back to being hairless."

"Some women like their men hairy."

"I like mine not to shed all over the cottage."

I wondered how Jericho would fare in the aftermath of the spell. Somehow, I didn't hold out hope for the loyal assistant. Veronica seemed to be set in her ways.

Veronica.

The seer's prediction had arguably been accurate. The realization did little to comfort me. If she was right about the spell, was she right about the horrible visions she'd seen when she tried to do my reading? I pushed it from my mind.

Stroking the back of his neck, I said, "You're wrong

about your inner animal, you know. You may have looked like a wolf, but you didn't act like one."

He grinned. "I peed outside, and I ate raw steak. How is that not acting like one?"

"That's surface level stuff. Your internal self didn't succumb to your external one. You didn't feel so much like an animal inside that you attacked anyone or acted on your baser instincts."

"I guess that's true."

Alec hadn't fared as well. Neither had a few others. They'd taken one look in the mirror and *became* their inner selves. What if it had been the same for the killer? What if their reflection had been a glimpse of their inner turmoil and, in the initial flare of the spell, they'd acted on it?

"Great gods above." My whole body stiffened as the pieces clicked into place.

"What is it?" Granger asked.

I pulled back to look at him. "I think I know who killed Bertram Lapp." I revealed my suspicion.

"Then let's go," Granger said, fully in sheriff mode now.

"I don't know where to find him at this hour. He could be home or still at work."

The sheriff mulled it over. "I'll have Pitt meet me at his house. You go with Bolan to his office."

"You heard the leprechaun. I'm not interrupting Bolan's dinner."

I'm coming, too. Raoul popped up from behind a bush.

I turned to glare at the Peeping Raoul. *Have you been spying on us the whole time?*

The raccoon shrugged. *There was nothing on television.*

"I'll take Raoul instead," I said.

"Sure, that's the same," Granger said with a faint trace of sarcasm.

"I'm going to his office," I said. "There's bound to be co-workers still there. I'll be far from alone."

"Fine, but don't do anything reckless."

I crossed my fingers at my side. "I wouldn't dream of it."

We parted ways at the cottage. I drove to the business complex and was pleased to see at least a dozen cars in the parking lot. Plenty of bodies should the suspect try to fight or flee.

I checked the listing on the wall until I found the right name. Third floor. Corner office. No surprise there.

The elf behind the front desk stopped us on our way to the elevator bank. "Sorry. No raccoons."

Raoul's outraged expression was lost on the elf.

"Is this rule specific to raccoons or is it any woodland creature?" I asked.

"We had an incident last year with a raccoon and a pizza party," the elf explained.

I've never seen this place in my life, I swear. He glanced to the left. *Although that statue does look vaguely familiar.* He scampered backward. *I think I'll wait outside.*

Sighing, I walked to the elevator bank alone. The doors opened, and worker bees spilled out of the car, finished for the day. I rode the elevator to the third floor. The corridor was deserted. It seemed I'd arrived during the mass office exodus.

The fairy was seated at his desk, staring intently at the mountain of paperwork in front of him. He definitely took after his father.

I knocked on the doorjamb. "Jeremiah, do you have a minute?"

It took a moment for him to register my presence. "Oh, it's you."

"Ember," I reminded him.

He waved me over. "Come in. I guess you're here about the spell." He smiled broadly. "Isn't it great? No more bloodshot eyes."

"It's good news for everybody." I paused. "Except your father, of course."

Jeremiah's face clouded over. "I don't know what you mean. The spell didn't kill my father. It certainly can't bring him back."

"It's funny. You're the only one who suggested that the spell might've targeted your father," I said. "At the time it seemed far fetched, but now I realize it was your guilt talking. You already knew the spell had targeted him. You just didn't expect it to impact everybody else in Starry Hollow."

Jeremiah feigned ignorance. "That's lunacy. Why would I feel any guilt? I had nothing to do with what happened."

I gave him my fiercest look, the one I used to reserve for men trying to stop me from repossessing their cars. The one that said, *Jersey Girl: Approach With Caution.*

"Your eyes weren't red because you saw yourself as tired and overworked," I told him. "They were a reflection of your inner anger and resentment."

"Anger? Resentment?" He scoffed. "Look around you. I have a pretty good life. What would I have to be angry about?"

"You resent your brother, and you were angry that your father didn't seem to see Timothy the way you did. You bought that spell from Enid in the hope that it would open your father's eyes to see the real Timothy, the one you see. Maybe it would encourage him to change his will, or at least leave you Timothy's half of the orchard instead of dividing Bertram's half between you and your brother."

He scowled. "You think I care about money? I have a

great job with benefits. Timothy's the one who's desperate for money. You should be talking to him. He had the most to gain from Dad's death. Now he doesn't have to worry about finding a job. He'll get money for doing absolutely nothing."

"And that really upsets you, doesn't it? You, the good son who handles everything. The one who plans parties, but still splits the credit with his useless brother. The one who does everything right but isn't any more loved by his father than the brother who does everything wrong."

Despite the broken spell, the rage returned to Jeremiah's eyes. He clenched his hands into fists and pounded on the desk. "Can you blame me? I work my wings off to prove myself day in and day out. Timothy causes us nothing but headaches, but we're still getting the same amount of the estate? This was his chance to change it. To show me I deserved more, but nope. He left it the same." The fairy radiated anger.

"How did you know? Did your father tell you?"

"He told us from a young age what his intentions were, but after Mom died, my dad had to update his will. I thought for sure that he'd finally see how unfair it was to split it equally. I thought if I could do a spell at his birthday that forced him to see Timothy for who he truly is, that he'd change his mind."

Jeremiah was right about one thing. It wasn't about money for him, not really. It was about approval. Validation. In wanting his father to see Timothy as he truly was, Jeremiah wanted his father to see *him* too. And to reward his lifetime of good behavior. I didn't have a sibling, yet I understood Jeremiah's desire to be seen and appreciated. But there was one key factor he got wrong.

"He never would've changed his mind, Jeremiah. Your father didn't need a spell to see your brother as he really is.

He saw. He just didn't care because he loved you both regardless. It's called unconditional love for a reason."

Jeremiah didn't seem to like my response. He pounded his fists again. "He should've cared! It should matter that I did everything right. Tim never put anybody else first. It was all about playing drums and screwing around, like he's ten years old."

"You didn't put everybody else first, though," I countered. "Think about it. By trying to please your father, you were putting yourself first. You wanted to be number one in his eyes, and you decided the best way to do that was to make your brother look bad."

"I didn't have to make Tim look bad. He did that all by himself," Jeremiah said bitterly.

I met his angry gaze. "If you really believe that, then why bother with the spell?"

"I just wanted my dad to see Timothy the way I do," he whispered.

"What happened when the spell hit?" I asked.

His eyes turned downcast. "I didn't mean to kill him. I sprayed the potion, and it was chaos. I wasn't expecting that. Everybody ran out of the room like the place was on fire. I checked with my father that he was okay—I was worried about another asthma attack—but did he even look at me? No, he immediately asked 'Where's Timothy?' *That* was his concern in the heat of the moment." Jeremiah shook his head ruefully. "I felt this overwhelming surge of anger, and I snapped. I grabbed him by the neck and started choking him. It was like an out-of-body experience. It didn't feel like me doing it."

"But it was you, Jeremiah. Your spell. Your actions." He wasn't the good son he believed himself to be.

"You can't prove it. You have no evidence."

"Your confession will take care of that." *You're my witness, Raoul. He confessed.*

Doesn't the witness need to be present? came the reply.

It's a contemporaneous statement. I saw it on television.

"Not if I take care of you first," Jeremiah seethed.

The fairy took me by surprise, flying across the desk at me. He wrapped his hands around my neck and began to throttle me.

"Your signature move, huh?" I choked out. Probably best not to antagonize the killer.

We toppled backward, and even then he managed to keep his grip on my neck. I couldn't breathe. I clawed at his hands, shocked by his strength.

I brought my knee to his groin. The pain was only enough to loosen his grip for a second. Fog invaded my head. I couldn't think straight.

Raoul, I called. I couldn't remember our safety word.

I tried to grab the leg of the nearby chair, intending to club Jeremiah with it. My fingers couldn't quite reach it. I knew I was about to pass out. I couldn't let that happen. If I blacked out now, Jeremiah would make sure I never woke up. Just like his father.

A growl interrupted my woeful thoughts. A giant ball of fur pounced on the fairy, pushing him off me. The creature was much too large to be Raoul.

I rolled to my side.

Granger.

The wolf pinned Jeremiah to the floor. I crawled across the floor to my purse and rifled through it in search of my wand.

"You'd think it would be sticking out, but noooo," I rasped. My throat was sore. Murphy's Law said that it'd be buried at the bottom with the packet of tissues and the empty tin of mints.

The wolf gave me a look that suggested he'd really like me to wrap this up. Although I didn't need my wand to perform magic, it helped me to control it. With Ivy's magic in the mix and Veronica's fearful words swimming in my head, I didn't want to risk messing up the spell. There'd been plenty of that in recent days.

As the wolf turned back to his prey, Jeremiah stole my move and seized the chair leg. He brought the piece of furniture down on the wolf's back. My heart squeezed as the wolf's body slid to the floor.

My eager fingers latched onto my wand, and I yanked it from its hiding spot, aiming it at Jeremiah. My head was still a little fuzzy as I grasped for a spell. *"Glacio! Congelo!* Whatever the word is for freeze."

Jeremiah's body grew stiff. I dashed across the room to check on Granger.

I'm here, but I've got an extra tail! Raoul's voice sliced through the fog in my head.

I had no idea what the raccoon meant until he rushed into the room with the elf from the lobby hot on his heels.

The elf skidded to a halt at the sight of a frozen Jeremiah and a limp wolf. "How did a wolf get past me?"

"It's Sheriff Nash," I said.

"Oh, right." The elf's head bobbed. "I let him in."

"The sheriff's going to arrest Jeremiah now," I explained.

"You might want to thaw him first, or he'll be hard to carry out," the elf suggested. "The ice adds extra weight."

I stared at him. "Thanks." I decided not to ask how he knew that. As far as I was concerned, there'd been enough revelations for one day.

Chapter Twenty-One

Retro Rollers was teeming with families as Marley and I approached the rink.

"You can't go out there without these."

I turned around to see Granger in his father's cowboy hat, holding up two pairs of skates.

"Where are yours?" I asked.

He looked down. I followed his gaze to the floor where he sported a pair of white skates with flashing blue lights.

"Fancy. You wear them well."

He kissed my cheek. "Thank you."

Marley and I sat on a bench to change into our skates. We held hands as we inched our way to the rink. Once inside, Marley gripped the ledge that circled the rink, continuing to squeeze my hand.

"How do you want to do this?" I asked.

She took a deep breath and released my hand. I spread my arms wide to stay balanced, keeping one eye trained on Marley as she let go. I felt a rush of pride when she joined the line of skaters as they passed by.

Granger rolled onto the rink. "Give her space, broomstick mama."

"I am. Trust me, I have no plans to skate after her."

He pulled me into a tight embrace. "It feels so good to do this again."

I buried my face in the fabric of his shirt. "One hundred percent agree." I sniffed. "You still smell like wolf though." I tipped my head back to look at him. "Not that it's a bad thing."

He grinned. "Glad to hear it."

"Unless you're wet. Then it's another smell entirely."

He kissed the tip of my nose, then migrated to my lips.

I broke off the kiss. "By any chance, can you roll your tongue?"

"Is it a dealbreaker if I can't?"

"Not at all. Pretty sure we've bumped up against every dealbreaker there could possibly be at this point."

"I'm relieved to hear you say that because there's a question I've been wanting to ask you."

My heart skipped a beat as I remembered the velvet box in his drawer. "Yes?"

He frowned. "Maybe not yet. Now that we're here, I'm not sure this is the right setting."

"You and I are in a room together, and neither one of us is dead, and there's no dead body. Trust me, this is the right setting."

He skated to the middle of the rink and beckoned for me to join him. As Marley glided past me, she gave me a gentle push. I went sailing across the rink toward my future.

Granger caught me before I rolled past him. Taking my hand, he got down on one knee, which wasn't easy on skates.

"Should I take off the hat first?" he asked.

"No," I said. "It suits you."

He squeezed my hand. "Ember Yarrow Rose."

"Just Ember."

He grinned. "Just Ember, will you make me the happiest werewolf in the history of the pack?"

"I think you're forgetting something," I said.

"Oh, right." As he reached into his pocket, I braced myself for the moment of truth. Maybe I wouldn't look at the ring. I'd look past it, at Granger. Then I wouldn't react. The last thing I wanted was for Granger to think my horrified reaction was to the proposal itself.

"The ring doesn't matter," I blurted.

He frowned. "You don't want a ring?"

I waved a hand in front of me. "Sorry. Carry on. I interrupted."

"Ember Rose, will you do me the great honor of marrying me?"

I surprised both of us by bursting into tears.

"Those are happy tears, right?" he asked, uncertain. "Please say yes."

"Yes," I croaked. "Happy."

The crowd of families cheered, and the rink lights flashed in a rainbow of colors, but I wasn't so blinded by them that I couldn't see the circle of gold that glinted in the palm of his hand. Embedded in the band were rubies designed to look like roses.

"It's beautiful," I whispered.

"You sound surprised."

"Of course not. I trust you." As I bent down to kiss him, I lost my balance. He caught me before I fell, and I came to rest on his thigh.

Marley skated out to join us, carting Raoul behind her in a mini sleigh. He didn't seem to mind the ride.

"Congratulations, Mom." She tried to hug me. Big mistake. We both lost our balance and crashed onto the floor, taking Granger with us. My bones hurt, but I couldn't stop laughing.

"That's going to bruise," Granger said, rubbing his hip.

"Living with her, it'll be the first of many," Marley quipped.

Skaters returned to circling the rink. We took our time getting back on our feet, just enjoying the moment, filling our buckets with joy. There was no rush. After all, we'd have the rest of our lives together.

Later that evening, Granger drove to his mother's house to share our good news. Marley left the skating rink to meet up with a group of friends, and Raoul disappeared into the woods, I suspected to pay an overdue visit to the dump.

"Looks like it's just you and me, bud," I told PP3. The dog didn't stir. I shoved my ring underneath his nose. "I'm engaged, by the way. It's pretty, right?" Now that I had it, I felt ridiculous for being overly concerned with the ring. I attributed it to prewedding jitters. I'd never been materialistic. I was more like Timothy Lapp when it came to material possessions.

Thank goodness Starry Hollow was back to paranormal, and another murder had been solved. With the spell broken, Linnea was able to reopen Palmetto House. Although I felt sad for residents like Artemis, Jericho, and Deputy Bolan, it didn't really matter how they appeared to others, only how they viewed themselves. I was relieved for Delphine, and to have human Granger back. As much as I loved the wolf side of him, it made conversations difficult. Unfortunately, I didn't share the same telepathic connection with Wolf Granger that I shared with Raoul, which was probably a good thing given the thoughts that sometimes crossed my mind.

I left PP3 on the bed and entered the bathroom to get ready for bed. I brushed my hair, grateful to see the dark strands shining under the harsh glare of the artificial lights. I wasn't sure when my hair had returned to normal. It definitely took longer to change, which was strange. Nobody else's recovery was delayed that I knew of. Typical me. Late to the party. Now that I knew how I looked as an almost blonde, though, I was willing to switch to a lighter shade once the white hairs started cropping up—but today was not that day.

As I set the brush on the counter, I heard a cracking sound. I stood perfectly still, listening closely to identify the source.

"PP3, did you eat cauliflower again?"

My question was followed by more cracking and, this time, even louder. I turned to the full-length mirror affixed to the back of the bathroom door. Hairline cracks had formed across the glass in the shape of an X.

"What the hell?"

I leaned closer to examine the fissures. What would cause that to happen? I heard a snapping sound and reeled back as the glass shifted.

The mirror cracked.

Shards of glass rained to the floor, forcing me backward. I stared in horrified silence as a woman emerged from the blank space. The same woman whose shadow I'd seen in the forest during my night flight. The same woman whose reflection had stared back at me in the powder room at Haverford House. Not just any woman.

Ivy Rose.

My infamous ancestor stepped daintily over the sharp debris. She stretched her arms over her head and paused to admire herself in the mirror over the sink. "My, that was quite a long break. I'm well rested now; I'll say that much for me." She whirled toward me, smiling. "I see congratulations are in order." She grabbed my hand to admire the ring. "He did well. I must admit, I was worried it might be an antique." She used air quotes around the word "antique." "But you know what they say, one woman's trashy ring is another woman's treasure."

I continued to gawk at her, unable to process what was happening. It simply wasn't possible. Ivy Rose had been dead for centuries.

"Silly me, a Rose should never forget her common courtesies. Thank you *so* much for all your help. I couldn't have done it without you. I would've been more than happy to use Marley, of course, but you've proven yourself stronger and more capable than I would've guessed. Who knew? And my garden..." She mimed a chef's kiss. "It's thriving, just like the old days. You two have been a gift from the gods."

I couldn't seem to form words. "How?" was all I managed.

"You haven't figured it out yet?" She clucked her tongue. "My magic has been slowly building inside you, coalescing, if you will. When the time was right, I steered you and your trash panda toward the spells I needed for my revival."

Revival was an interesting word choice.

She plucked my toothbrush from the holder and examined the bristles. "You don't mind if I borrow this, do you? My breath must be rancid after all this time. Limbo wreaks havoc on the system. I almost wreaked havoc on you, too."

She shuddered. "Your hair was a catastrophe. I'm glad I was able to sort everything out and make a clean break. I had no desire to merge bodies." She looked me up and down. "No offense. To be fair, yours isn't half bad."

"The summoning spell," I said, more to myself.

"And the necromancy. Don't forget that one. I wasn't convinced you'd go through with it, but a girl has to try." She booped my nose with the end of the toothbrush. "It helped that my magic was all concentrated in one place." She patted my shoulder. "I'll have to figure out how to extract the rest of it from you, but that's a problem for Future Ivy. Now, do be a good witch and fetch my wand, Yarrow. For the night is young, and I hath revenge to wreak."

You don't want to miss **Magic & Mistletoe**, the next book in the Starry Hollow Witches series.

Manufactured by Amazon.ca
Bolton, ON